KU-366-193

WITHDRAWN
FROM STOCK

2 1 JUL 2010

'You wanted to talk about ground rules.' Khalid's voice was a rich drawl. 'I agree. It's well past time for that.'

The intensity of his stare held her taut and breathless as her heartbeat thudded, loud in her ears. Something had changed. Treacherous undercurrents swirled between them.

'Perhaps we could work the details out tomorrow. It's getting late.' Her words tumbled out in a rush. Maggie felt strangely vulnerable in this highly charged atmosphere.

'There's no need to wait until tomorrow,' he murmured.

'There isn't?' Maggie watched him stride around the desk, each movement slow and purposeful. She found herself turning so her back was to the desk and Khalid stood between her and the door. Tremors of shock vibrated through her. And something else. A tiny thrill of excitement. She must be mad!

'No,' he said, his voice a deep rumble. 'We'll sort this out tonight.'

Her eyes were lustrous gold in the lamplight, shot with emerald fire. Khalid had never known any like them. Her chest rose and fell rapidly, her breasts thrusting in wanton invitation against the fabric. Her lips parted as her breaths shortened.

His body tensed to the point of pain as he prolonged the suspense of anticipation a moment more. He'd never been one to rush his pleasure.

And Maggie would be pure pleasure.

Annie West spent her childhood with her nose between the covers of a book—a habit she retains. After years of preparing government reports and official correspondence she decided to write something she *really* enjoys. And there's nothing she loves more than a great romance. Despite her office-bound past she has managed a few interesting moments—including a marriage offer with the promise of a herd of camels to sweeten the contract. She is happily married to her ever-patient husband (who has never owned a dromedary). They live with their two children amongst the tall eucalypts at beautiful Lake Macquarie, on Australia's east coast. You can e-mail Annie at www.annie-west.com, or write to her at PO Box 1041, Warners Bay, NSW 2282, Australia.

Recent books by the same author:

THE GREEK TYCOON'S UNEXPECTED WIFE

THE DESERT KING'S PREGNANT BRIDE

BY
ANNIE WEST

MILLS & BOON®
Pure reading pleasure™

All the characters in this book have no existence outside the imagination of the author, and have no relation whatsoever to anyone bearing the same name or names. They are not even distantly inspired by any individual known or unknown to the author, and all the incidents are pure invention.

All Rights Reserved including the right of reproduction in whole or in part in any form. This edition is published by arrangement with Harlequin Enterprises II BV/S.à.r.l. The text of this publication or any part thereof may not be reproduced or transmitted in any form or by any means, electronic or mechanical, including photocopying, recording, storage in an information retrieval system, or otherwise, without the written permission of the publisher.

® and TM are trademarks owned and used by the trademark owner and/or its licensee. Trademarks marked with ® are registered with the United Kingdom Patent Office and/or the Office for Harmonisation in the Internal Market and in other countries.

First published in Great Britain 2008
Harlequin Mills & Boon Limited,
Eton House, 18-24 Paradise Road, Richmond, Surrey TW9 1SR

© Annie West 2008

ISBN: 978 0 263 20341 7

Set in Times Roman 10½ on 11½ pt
07-0808-52584

Printed and bound in Great Britain
by Antony Rowe Ltd, Chippenham, Wiltshire

THE
DESERT KING'S
PREGNANT BRIDE

With warmest gratitude to:
Leanne McMahon, equine expert extraordinaire;
Anna Campbell, the best friend a girl could have;
and my very own hero, Geoff.
Thank you.
This book wouldn't have been possible without you!

CHAPTER ONE

MAGGIE bowed her head against the sheets of icy rain as she plodded along the muddy road.

Slick fabric stuck to her where she'd forgotten to do up her raincoat. Water sluiced down her legs, into her wellington boots. Her hair, so carefully washed and dried, now hung in saturated rat-tails against her neck. Vaguely she was aware of the chill numbing her body. After running, stumbling, then trudging so far in the lashing darkness, her steps slowed, became unsteady.

If she'd been thinking clearly, she'd have taken her battered Jeep. That hadn't occurred to her. One look between the carelessly drawn curtains of Marcus's sitting room and coherent thought had fled.

She'd stood, rooted to the spot, heedless of the drenching rain. When her brain had finally caught up with the message her eyes had conveyed, she'd simply run. She must have raced past her car into the welcoming blackness.

Pain tore at her throat as she sobbed in a deep racking breath. She had to get home, before the emotions churning inside overcame her.

Yet she couldn't escape the memory of what she'd seen: Marcus, naked in the arms of his lover.

Now she understood why he'd blown hot and cold, sometimes too busy to see her and at others attentive and loving. His affection had been a sham. He'd only wanted her to conceal his affair with the trophy wife of a jealous horse breeder.

Maggie's stomach churned. She'd been so gullible.

She'd believed him when he'd spoken of respecting her, not rushing her after her recent loss. He'd said she needed to be sure before they took their relationship further.

In her innocence Maggie *had* been sure. She'd decided to show him she was a desirable woman, mature and ready for a deeper relationship. She'd read every magazine she could lay her hands on, aiming to transform herself into the sort of woman she thought he wanted. She'd overcome her fears and thrust aside self-doubt. She'd even taken the long trip to town and bought herself a *dress*!

Her bitter laughter was swallowed by the rushing wind.

He'd never wanted her. She'd been too inexperienced and starved of affection to see he was using her. Nausea welled in her throat and she bent over to dry-retch again.

Strangely, this time as she looked down she could see her boots and her legs, wet and muddy below the raincoat. She frowned muzzily, trying to focus on the present, not the scene of contorting naked bodies replaying in her head.

Where was the light coming from?

'Do you need help?' A deep voice curled out of the roaring darkness to reach her.

Blindly, she raised her head and found herself blinking in the headlights of a massive off-road vehicle. A man stood silhouetted before it. He was tall, lean and unfamiliar. Something about the set of his broad shoulders and his wide-planted feet intimated he was a man prepared for anything, a man able to deal with trouble of any kind.

Maggie knew an instant's insane craving to lean forward into his strong body, rest against those more-than-capable shoulders and slump into oblivion.

Then sense overcame instinct. She had no idea who he was. Besides, she'd just learned her judgement was fatally flawed.

She'd believed Marcus to be everything she wanted in a man, a lover, a mate. She'd thought…

The shadow moved closer, near enough to make her stunningly aware of his superior height and power.

'You're not well. How can I assist?' This time Maggie caught the faintest trace of an accent.

'Who are you?' she said, barely recognising the reedy whisper as her own voice.

Silence for a moment as the wind stirred the collar of her coat and drove the rain almost horizontal.

'I'm a guest at the Tallawanta Stud. Staying up at the homestead.'

Now she recognised the latest top-of-the-range vehicle. Only the best for those at the big house. And there was a special guest this week. The Sheikh of Shajehar, who owned the whole enormous horse stud, had sent an envoy on an inspection tour.

That explained his accent. The precise, clipped English, as if he'd attended a top British public school. It was overlaid with a slight softening of consonants that hinted at something far more exotic.

'Or do you intend that we both stand out here till we're saturated to the skin?'

There was no impatience in that voice, but nor was there any mistaking its steely undertone. Maggie jumped, reining in her wandering thoughts. What was wrong with her? She couldn't seem to concentrate properly.

Only now did she realise the stranger wore no overcoat. He must be even wetter than she.

'I'm sorry.' She shook her head dazedly. 'I'm not…'

'Have you been in an accident?' Again that easy, calm voice with just a hint of iron in its depths.

'No. No accident. I… Could you give me a lift, please?' Maggie had no qualms now about cadging a ride from him. He was the visiting dignitary she'd heard about. They were on the estate's private road and no one would be out in this weather unless they belonged here.

'Of course.' He bowed his head, then preceded her to the four-wheel drive. His stride was long, purposeful and easy, as if pacing down a carpeted corridor instead of a muddy, uneven gravel road. Maggie stumbled after him as best she could, her limbs horribly uncoordinated.

He opened the door and stood back for her to get in.

'Thank you,' she murmured as a firm hand cupped her elbow and helped her into the high cabin. Without his support she wouldn't have made it.

Maggie subsided onto the cushioned seat. Slowly she loosened her cramped fingers and let go of the straps of her high-heeled sandals from one hand, her frivolous new purse from the other. They tumbled to the floor. She'd barely been aware she still held them.

The door closed and she sank back, stunned by the warm comfort of the cabin after the howling wind and teeming rain that had drummed incessantly in her ears.

This was…luxury. Heaven.

Maggie shut her eyes, overcome by the quiet peace.

'Here,' a deep voice filtered into her consciousness, 'take this.'

Slowly she turned towards the velvet-soft voice, fighting the intense dragging weariness that consumed her. She didn't want to rouse herself, but he was insistent.

Reluctantly, she opened her eyes. He sat in the driver's seat and she looked up into the blackest eyes she'd ever seen. Deep-set, hooded eyes that surveyed her closely, taking in every nuance of her appearance.

Maggie's eyes widened at the sight of her rescuer in the cabin's pale overhead light.

His jet-black hair was slicked back from a face tanned almost to bronze. Her breath snagged at the strong, spare beauty of his features, each plane emphasised by the sheen of rain on burnished flesh. Lean cheeks with slanted cheekbones that mirrored the stark angle of his brows. A strong, aristocratic nose with just a hint of the aquiline. Narrow, well-shaped lips that she could imagine tipping into a smile or turning down in displeasure. A jaw that spoke of solid power and bone-deep assurance.

The combination took her breath away. It was as if someone had opened a precious old book and conjured a warrior prince straight from the *Arabian Nights*.

But nothing in her juvenile reading matched this man for pure magnetism. He looked exotic and masterful.

Maggie had never known any man could look so…

'Here,' he repeated, thrusting a soft woollen blanket into her hands. His brows angled down in a frown as he surveyed her. 'Are you sure you're not injured?'

She nodded, then hid her face in the folds of wool, holding the blanket with hands that trembled. Embarrassment washed through her, whether because he'd caught her staring, or because of her strange wayward thoughts, she didn't know.

She must be in shock. That would explain her heedless flight and the muzzy feeling that everything was distant, unreal. Yes, that was it. Shock.

Any woman would be shocked to discover what she had tonight. And no doubt she looked a sight: workaday raingear over her beaded dress—

'Stop it.' A firm hand curved around her jaw and swung her face towards him. His fingers were hard and warm and comfortingly real against her numb flesh.

Maggie blinked, amazed to discover the water spiking her lashes wasn't rain, but tears. They burned her eyes.

'Stop what?' she whispered on a hiccough, staring into liquid dark eyes that held hers mesmerised.

Gradually her galloping heartbeat slowed. The breath shuddered out of her constricted lungs. She dragged in air, conscious of a tight ache around her chest.

'You were becoming hysterical.'

His clasp of her chin shifted, fingers splaying wide to tilt her head higher as if he needed to see her better in the dim light. The heat of his touch burned life back into her frozen skin and she was content to let him hold her so. She felt strangely lethargic.

'S-s-sorry.' She frowned. She'd never stuttered in her life. And as for being hysterical… 'I've had a bit of a sh-shock.' There, she finally got it out. She had trouble coordinating her lips and tongue. 'I'll be all r-right.'

'You've been out in this storm too long.' He took the wool from her white-knuckled grasp and lifted the blanket around her shoulders, pulling the edges together. The enveloping comfort relaxed her into a boneless huddle and the movement drew him close. She caught his scent, faint yet intriguing. Heat and sandalwood, spice and damp male skin. Her nostrils flared as she slumped forward.

Large hands on her shoulders propped her away from him.

'Where did you come from? How long have you been out?'

Maggie's lips curved up in a dreamy smile as her eyelids drifted lower. She really did love that accent. The softening consonants and lilting rhythm almost hidden behind the crisp intonation sounded quite…seductive. She could imagine going to sleep to the sound of that voice.

Her eyes popped open as fingers curled hard into her shoulders.

'Did someone hurt you?' His voice sounded different. She shivered anew at the hint of anger in his tone.

'No! No, I'm fine. Just…' The words petered out and she blinked, confused. She really did feel odd. 'I need to g-g-get back. Please.'

Abruptly, he nodded, pushing her back into the moulded seat and reaching for her seat belt. The heat of his torso as he leant near was warmer by far than any blanket.

'Where to?'

He straightened and immediately the chill invaded her body again. When he switched on the ignition the cabin was plunged into darkness but for the light from the control panel. Her gaze strayed to his shadowy profile: powerful yet elegant in a toughly masculine way.

Instinct told her she could trust him absolutely.

'Another s-s-six k-kilometres. Then r-right. I'll direct you f-from there.'

He eased the vehicle forward. Rain pounded on the roof and the four-wheel drive slid in the thick mud.

Mud. Her boots. Her gaze spanned the interior of the luxury vehicle.

'I'm sorry,' she whispered. 'My b-boots are f-filthy.'

'This is a farm vehicle,' he responded. 'I'm sure it collects its fair share of mud.'

Spoken like a man who never had to clean said vehicle, Maggie realised. This was no work vehicle. It was reserved for important guests, used when only the best would do.

'Who are you?'

For a moment she thought he hadn't heard her question over the sound of the rain.

'My name is Khalid. And yours?'

'Maggie.' She hugged the blanket closer, 'Maggie Lewis.' Thank goodness her teeth had stopped chattering.

'I'm pleased to meet you, Maggie.' His voice was grave, almost formal. Suddenly she wondered how this man spent his time when he wasn't visiting Australian horse studs or rescuing stranded women from deserted roads.

Khalid concentrated on the road as driving conditions deteriorated. He had to get her warm and dry quickly. She was in shock and might be on the verge of hypothermia.

Six kilometres and then how far to reach her destination? He couldn't take that risk. Instead he'd drive her to Tallawanta till she recovered.

She was an enigma. There was no abandoned car and those weren't work clothes beneath her oilskin. The glimpse of long slender legs below her coat had instantly caught his interest. And the high heels she'd dangled from her hand were for dancing the night away or seducing a man.

Was that what had happened? Had some man hurt her?

Despite her height, tall enough to top his shoulder, there was a fragile air about this woman. Her shadowed eyes were huge in that milky pale face. Her bowed neck as she'd hunched over in the road was long and slender and delicate.

She hadn't been at tonight's dinner of luminaries who'd turned out to meet the heir to the throne of Shajehar. Khalid would have noticed.

He flicked a glance at her, huddled beneath the tartan rug, her eyes closed and her head lolling against the seat. She looked weak and defenceless, but she must have a core of gritty strength to head out in this weather on foot. The woman was an intriguing mix that triggered his curiosity. That hadn't happened in a long time.

He felt a spurt of satisfaction that tonight, for once, he was without his entourage of security aides and obsequious hosts. He could indulge his curiosity, follow his instincts. Given the tight perimeter security on the vast estate, he'd won the argument that he was safe alone within its boundaries. Perhaps his security chief had realised too that it would be wise to give him space.

For six weeks Khalid had dutifully toured his half-brother's royal holdings in Europe, the Americas and Australia. But he didn't share Faruq's enjoyment of pomp and luxury. As heir to his terminally ill half-brother, Khalid had recently acquired a huge security retinue. Its size was due to Faruq's love of ostentation rather than any threat. Plus he had a schedule full of social engagements.

Social engagements! His time would be better spent supervising his latest project, a fresh water pipeline from the mountains in remote Shajehar. At least that would bring tangible benefits to his people.

Lights shone ahead in the streaming darkness and the tension eased across his shoulders and arms. Once he got her inside, in the light and warmth, he could assess her injuries, call a doctor if need be.

He bypassed the garages and drove round to the private owner's wing of the sprawling homestead.

'Here we are.' He leaned across to shake her awake. She was limp beneath his hand. Frowning, he paused only a moment before touching her pale cheek. It was icy.

'Maggie! Wake up.'

That voice again. The crisp warm voice with its tantalising hint of a lilt. She smiled to herself as she pictured an exotic prince in flowing robes, a gleaming scimitar in his hand.

'Maggie!'

She shrugged off a hand that threatened to interrupt her lovely dream. In her mind her prince smiled and tugged her to him. Eyes brighter than gems gleamed down at her and her breath caught. He slipped his hand beneath her legs and lifted her in his embrace, his arms like cushioned steel.

She'd never felt so safe, so secure, so full of anticipation. Those black eyes were shadowed with the promise of unknown delight, his narrow lips curving in a knowing, sensuous smile that made her long for his kiss.

The steady drum of his heartbeat pulsed against her and his arms rocked her close as he strode over the warm sand. Soon now they'd—

Maggie's brows pleated as hard drops of water beat against her face. Did it rain in the desert?

Instinctively, she turned her head, snuggling closer to his warm, solid body, filling her nostrils with the evocative scent of man. But her frown grew as she discovered he was wet, his clothes sodden.

She opened her eyes and found herself in a man's arms as he strode through a howling rainstorm. Her startled gasp was torn away by the wind.

Carriage lights shone along the veranda of a classic-style colonial homestead. Warm light gleamed through a massive fanlight window above the door. Suddenly everything clicked into place. Marcus, the long walk home, the exotic stranger. They were at Tallawanta House.

'You can put me down.' Maggie tried to lever herself up and out of his hold but she could get no purchase.

'We're almost there.' He stepped under cover and the needling rain on her skin ceased abruptly.

Wordlessly he pushed open the front door, pulling her closer. Muffled against his chest, she was assailed again by that yearning. To stay here against him, his body warming hers. To discover more about the inexplicable excitement that shivered through her blood when he held her like this.

She squeezed her eyes shut. This was no fantasy. This was real. Yet she felt oddly relaxed, almost floating. A yawn seized her and her head lolled against his shoulder.

Khalid. That was his name. She loved the sound of it. Her lips moved as she traced its syllables.

A moment later his grip changed, strong arms holding her flush against him as he lowered her legs. She slid down a hard torso till her feet reached the floor. Yet it was his unyielding embrace that kept her upright.

'Now,' murmured that seductively low voice, 'it's time to get your clothes off.'

'What?' Her eyes snapped open, instantly arresting him. In the bright light he found they were the colour of rich honey sprinkled with green fire. *Mesmerising.*

Unsteady hands shoved at his chest, fending him off.

Khalid's lips firmed as he watched her battle to remain upright. Had someone taken advantage of her tonight? The idea sent heat roaring through his blood.

'You need to get your wet clothes off.'

'Not with you watching!' Pink tinted her cheeks, fascinating him, highlighting a spattering of light freckles. A woman who still knew how to blush. When was the last time he'd come across one of that rare breed?

'I simply want to make sure you don't get hypothermia. I'm not interested in your body.'

The blush intensified to a deep rose hue and her gaze slanted swiftly away from his. Her teeth sank into her pale bottom lip. She was embarrassed.

'I can look after myself. I don't need your help,' she mumbled.

Didn't she? His curiosity was roused, and his concern. And, damn it, his time was his own, for tonight at least.

Khalid had always believed in two things. Following his instinct and his duty. Years ago, in the darkest days of grief after Shahina's death, only duty had kept him going. Embracing his responsibility to his people had given him purpose and strength when he'd wanted to shun the world and mourn his wife, the only woman he'd ever love.

Now both instinct and duty dictated he remain.

And something else. Something about Maggie Lewis that reached out to him in a way he hadn't experienced in a long time. The realisation fascinated and appalled him.

'So I should have left you out in the storm?'

'I didn't mean that. I appreciate the lift.' Her widening gaze roved the massive bathroom as if she'd never seen marble tiles before. 'It would have been easier to take me home.'

Her words were still slurred. But her eyes were clear and bright, the pupils normal. He guessed it was hypothermia, not drugs or drink, affecting her speech.

He released his hold slowly, looking to ensure she could

stand alone. Then he shrugged out of his dinner jacket and draped it over the edge of the spa bath.

Maggie watched his swift, economical movements as he turned and took off his jacket. The frame of his spectacular shoulders, the impressive V of his torso, the classic male form of powerful chest and narrow waist. The wet shirt clung lovingly to every inch of his skin, and her mouth dried, absorbing all that physical perfection.

Fiery heat burned her face as embarrassment sizzled under her skin. Of course he wasn't interested in seeing her naked! She'd always been gawky and unattractive. A wave of anger and humiliation broke over her, threatening to tug her down into a tide of self-pity.

Rapidly she blinked. She'd known for years she wasn't the sort of girl men desired. Tonight had only just confirmed...no, she refused to go there. The memory was too raw, too mortifying.

There was a whoosh of water and she dragged her focus back to the present. He'd leaned in to turn on the shower. His black trousers were sodden, shaping long, powerful legs and a tightly curved backside.

Maggie's eyes widened. Even Marcus, with his laughing blue eyes and his tall chunky build, couldn't hold a candle to this man for sheer physical perfection.

'Let me help you with your coat.' He didn't wait for an answer. Clearly he was used to being obeyed.

Wordlessly she stood while he deftly slipped it from her shoulders. It dropped in a puddle at her feet.

Maggie fixed her gaze on his black silk bow tie rather than on that vast expanse of wet male torso. But, perversely, the longer she stared, the greater her desire to reach out and tug the tie undone, to part the collar and see whether the flesh over his collarbone was the same burnished gold as his face.

Horrified at the wayward thought, she shut her eyes against

temptation. She'd never felt quite so…abandoned. Had tonight short-circuited something in her brain?

She was shocked to realise she hadn't felt anything like this for Marcus. She'd cared for him, respected him and believed intimacy was the next logical step in their relationship. But she'd never felt this charged awareness of him as a man.

Now she felt edgy, as if her skin had grown too tight.

Was this desire?

Her experience was so limited. She'd spent her life on the farm, isolated by her domineering father and long work hours. That was why her fledgling relationship with Marcus had seemed so precious.

'Next your dress, then we'll see if you can manage alone.' Khalid's voice was matter-of-fact. Yet he could have been reciting entries in the telephone directory and she'd have listened, enthralled, to his sexy smooth voice.

No! This had to stop. The sooner he left, the better. Then she'd become herself again: ordinary, pragmatic Maggie Lewis. No more flights of fantasy, no more…melting at the mere sound of a voice. This responsiveness to a complete stranger was due to shock and tiredness.

Maggie bit her lip on an instinctive protest as he reached round to the back of her dress. Her hands were so unsteady she knew she'd never manage the zip herself. So she complied, holding herself still as he tugged the zip.

Its downward slide took for ever. Blood pounded in her ears, blocking the sound of the shower. The sensation of the fastening lowering, centimetre by slow centimetre, drew her skin tight in goose flesh. He didn't touch her but he stood close, arms encircling her, his heat enfolding her.

She swayed then, horrified, caught herself and stood straighter, her spine ramrod stiff.

'There. Almost done.' His voice was expressionless, his eyes on the dress as he peeled it gently down.

He might have been undressing a store dummy for all the

interest he showed. And that, for some reason, was worse than anything that had gone before.

A shimmer of furious tears blurred Maggie's vision.

Here she stood, naked but for her brand-new ultra-feminine underwear, and he didn't even spare her a glance. It was as if she weren't a flesh-and-blood woman. Not a real one, capable of snaring a man's interest.

Who did she think she was kidding with her new clothes? Her body was too long, with too few curves. She had none of the sensuality other women took for granted.

The only time men noticed her was at work, for she was good at her job. In the stables she was one of the guys. Didn't that say it all? Something deep inside shrivelled up. An ache cramped her belly and she hunched over.

'Maggie? Are you in pain?' Eyes of fathomless black met hers. His hard, callused hands bit into her shoulders.

'No.' It emerged as a desperate gasp. 'But I need to be alone. Go. Please.'

His gaze raked hers. His mouth firmed into a grim line. Then slowly his fingers loosed their grip and his arms swung to his sides.

'As you wish.' Abruptly he was gone, leaving her in solitary possession of the magnificent bathroom.

For a bereft moment she wanted to call him back, ask him to hold her, to protect her from the hurt that welled up inside and the marrow-deep cold that gripped her body.

Then pride reasserted itself. He'd been only too thankful to escape. Besides, she was used to managing alone. That was the way it had always been.

She turned towards the shower, her steps as slow as an old woman's. She didn't bother to lock the door to ensure her privacy. There was no need.

Why did the knowledge hurt so much?

CHAPTER TWO

MAGGIE emerged from the bathroom swathed in soft white towelling, an oversized robe that swamped her. She hadn't even noticed Khalid take her discarded dress. The plush robe was warm against her damp skin. She hiked up the collar and dug her hands into the deep pockets.

For a heartbeat she hesitated in the doorway, then swung round at the sound of his voice.

'Feel better now?' Khalid halted a few paces away, legs planted wide in a stance that was intrinsically male. He surveyed her from top to toe. Her pulse hammered hard and loud. 'You look better. There's colour in your cheeks.'

And no wonder! Maggie felt the heat sizzle under her skin. She was uncomfortable wearing his robe, but it was all she had to hide her nakedness.

Under his survey the brush of fabric against her bare flesh suddenly took on a new dimension. Tingles rayed out from her sensitive breasts, her stomach, thighs and buttocks as she shifted her weight uneasily.

Or maybe it was reaction to the sight of him, clad in black trousers and black shirt that emphasised his spare, powerful frame. Her glance dropped all the way down past his muscled thighs to his bare feet. Her breath stopped. He even had sexy feet. She hadn't known that was possible.

Maggie snagged a desperate breath and jerked her gaze up to his, praying he hadn't noticed her ogling him.

'Thank you. I feel a lot better. Hot water works wonders, doesn't it?' Was she gabbling? For the first time since he found her, she felt truly nervous. She slicked her tongue over her bottom lip as her mouth dried.

'Come.' He held out his hand imperiously, and to her surprise, she reached out unhesitatingly. The hard heat of his palm and fingers enfolding hers was strangely comforting. If she could ignore the tendrils of shivery pleasure snaking up from their clasped hands.

He led her into a large sitting room. It should have been overpowering with its gilt-edged mirrors and elegant antique furniture. But it was lit by a fire in the grate and the mellow glow of lamps. The long sofa drawn up before the fire looked cosy with its many cushions and rich red throw rug.

'Sit.' He gestured to the sofa. 'It will be a while before your clothes dry and we can get you home. In the meantime you need to keep warm.'

As she subsided into the soft luxurious cushions Maggie knew there wasn't any danger of her growing cold. The hot shower, the fire, but most of all the way her blood heated at his touch, made her glow with warmth.

Wordlessly he covered her knees, then passed her a delicate glass in a filigree metal holder.

Maggie inhaled the steam rising from the glass. It smelt wonderful.

'What is it?'

'Sweet tea, Shajehani style. The perfect remedy for shock and exposure to the elements.' He stood before her, his back to the fire. Maggie drank in the sight of him, his imposing frame, his obvious strength, the stance of a man utterly confident and in control. Something squeezed the pit of her stomach. Hurriedly she bent her head to drink.

'It's delicious!'

'Surprising, isn't it?'

'No, I didn't mean—'

'It's all right. Drink up and relax. I'll be back soon.' He moved away and her breathing eased.

This was what she needed, to be alone to collect her thoughts and overcome these unfamiliar emotions that tonight ran so close to the surface.

She stared at the blazing fire, sipped her tea and wondered at the intensity of her reaction to Khalid. He was a stranger. A breathtakingly gorgeous one. Yet it wasn't just his looks she responded to. It was his easy kindness, that sense of rock-solid dependability, the way he took charge and looked after her as if it was the most natural thing in the world. She wasn't used to it.

Maggie blinked. She'd forgotten what it was like to feel cared for. To lean on someone else. No one had ever taken care of her like this. Not since she was eight and she'd arrived home from school to find her mother had walked out, taking Maggie's little sister, but not Maggie.

There'd been no warmth at home after that day. Her father hadn't been one for creature comforts, let alone a hug or a sympathetic smile. He'd been a hard man, dour and demanding. Even in those last months as she'd nursed him he hadn't softened.

'Is there anything else you need?' Khalid's deep voice came from beside her. She hadn't heard him return.

To her horror, the hint of concern lacing his words opened a floodgate of raw emotion. Painful emotion that ignited a terrible weakness in her. She wasn't accustomed to sympathy.

Her lips quivered. What was wrong with her? She'd discovered Marcus's betrayal and she'd got a soaking. It wasn't the end of the world.

She was made of sterner stuff than this. Maggie Lewis

never cried. It was one of the reasons she'd been accepted so quickly into the male realm of the horse stud.

'No.' The word emerged as a raw croak and she tried again. 'No, thank you.' She relinquished her stiff-knuckled grip on the glass as a large, tanned hand took it from her.

'In that case let's get your hair dry.'

Maggie opened her mouth to object, but already he'd draped a towel over her head and shoulders. Long, strong fingers massaged her scalp through the thick towelling and her demurral dissolved on her tongue.

Whorls of sensation spread from his supple hands, sensation that made the last of her resistance melt like chocolate on a hot summer day.

Her head lolled back and forward, following the easy rhythm of his hands, till she forgot what it was she objected to. Ripples of delight spread out, down her spine, across her shoulders and lower, deep inside her.

She had to stifle a sigh of regret when he lifted the towel away. It felt so good, the warmth, the company, the comfort of his presence.

She squeezed her eyes shut against the awful sensation of loss and loneliness welling inside her. The aching void of emptiness that stretched all around her.

Quickly she shook her head, hoping to dislodge the ache, the unfamiliar need. Tonight *had* been a shock, a blow to her self-esteem and her hopes, but she'd get over it. This curious sense of frailty was a passing thing. She'd always been strong. Always coped.

'Don't cry, little one.' His voice was so low it was a mere thread of sound, weaving into her consciousness. His touch was tender as he wiped moisture from her cheeks.

Maggie kept her eyes tight shut. For the second time tonight she had tears in her eyes. The second time in fifteen years. She hadn't cried since her mother had deserted her all those years ago. Maggie had sobbed herself sick then and hadn't cried since. Now in one night the dam had broken. A shudder of anxiety racked her.

'Please,' she whispered. 'I don't want to be alone.'

Khalid stared into the flames, legs outstretched in a casual pose that belied his inner turmoil. Tension pulled his shoulders tight and a charged sense of expectancy weighted his limbs.

Beside him Maggie sat with her feet curled beneath her. She was close enough for him to be aware of her every move and feel her beckoning warmth.

Yet he didn't touch her.

He fought his instinctive reaction to reach out and hold her, comfort her. He had more sense than that.

Just sitting here was a test of his willpower, and his honour. His desire to pull her into his embrace wasn't as altruistic as it should have been. Maybe bringing her here hadn't been wise after all.

Instead of leaping flames the picture filling his brain was Maggie Lewis, standing in his *en suite*, wearing nothing but lace underwear and pride. She'd been brave, beautiful and hurting, unable to hide the raw anguish in her remarkable eyes.

But it wasn't her eyes that had riveted his attention. Her lithe body was all elegant lines, pale skin that dipped and curved in exactly the right places. His hands had itched to reach out and take the weight of her high, proud breasts, to smooth over her narrow waist to the gentle curve of her hips. Hunger had surged in him so strongly that he'd been forced to leave the room, lest he do something unforgivable.

She'd looked so perfect, so pure, he could almost have believed her untouched.

Why was he imagining his hands, dark and hard, on her pristine flesh? He'd never fantasised about taking a virgin. His experience in that area was a lifetime ago.

His mind slammed shut on the old memory. There'd been

women since Shahina. Beautiful, clever, accommodating women who gave him the satisfaction his body craved. But never had his mind or his emotions been engaged. That was exactly how he wanted it. Short, easy relationships built on physical pleasure were no threat to his heart. That was how he'd lived his life since the death of his wife and it was precisely how he intended to continue.

He frowned, recognising that tonight, with Maggie Lewis, something was different. Sexual need was there, a scorching spike in his bloodstream. But something else too, more complex than physical desire. A shadow, a hint of something *more*. Something that stirred his emotions, as well as his libido. Something he had no wish to feel.

He dragged in a deep breath, trying not to notice the way her clean, feminine scent stirred his senses.

'Do you want to talk about it?' So much for his determination not to get involved.

He couldn't contain his curiosity about the intriguing woman so innocently sharing his couch.

He rubbed his jaw. He couldn't remember sharing anything innocently with a woman since Shahina.

'Did someone hurt you?' He'd make it his business to find the man and bring him to account.

'It was my fault,' she muttered, eyes downcast.

A chill iced his veins. 'Don't say that.'

'It's true. I was the one with expectations.'

'If some man forced himself on you after you'd changed your mind, it's not your fault.'

In the fire-lit shadows huge eyes met his. Her hands clenched tight together.

'No. You've got it all wrong.' Her words ended on a hiccough of unsteady laughter. 'No one forced himself on me.' Her voice was stronger, her mouth firm. 'I wasn't assaulted, if that's what you think.'

On a surge of movement she wriggled higher, squaring her slumped shoulders. Unfortunately the movement made the collar of the robe gape to reveal a sliver of pale, enticing flesh. Khalid moved restlessly and shifted his gaze. But despite the thick towelling he could easily visualise her pert breasts and smooth, silken skin.

He turned to the fire, trying to ignore the rapid thump of his pulse and the heat igniting in his loins.

'You don't need to worry. Untouched by the hand of man. That's me.' Her voice was bitter and hard.

'Pardon?' For a moment he was startled, remembering his fantasy of her as virginal, awaking to his caress. He realised how unlikely that was. She must be talking about tonight. He swung around, unable to resist temptation.

She looked different, more alive, more vibrant. A flush of colour tinted her cheeks and her eyes were bright.

His belly contracted hard as desire stabbed him. She'd got under his skin when she'd been pale and fragile. Now her features were animated, renewed energy evident in her taut body. She was far too alluring.

'Nothing happened tonight.' She lifted a dismissive hand. 'Nothing momentous, that is.' Her lips twisted in a tight grimace that belied her words.

Taking in the determined jut of her chin, he knew she lied. He gave her full marks for her valiant effort. But something *had* happened, even if it hadn't been rape.

'You said you'd had a shock.'

She shrugged, pursing her lips. 'Have you ever made an error of judgement?' she asked at last.

'Of course. Everyone has.'

'There's a comfort.' She paused. 'Well, I just made a mistake. A huge one.' She drew in a deep breath. Khalid fought to stop his gaze straying to the shadow of her cleavage. 'Tonight I found out just how stupid I'd been.'

Her words were defiant, her profile proud, yet Khalid had

seen her at rock-bottom just an hour ago. He knew she must still be hurting badly.

Over the past eight years countless women had tried to snare him with guile, seduction and emotional appeals. He'd remained unmoved. His heart had died with his wife and he had no intention of laying himself open to the raw pain of loss again. But his experience had taught him to distinguish female wiles at a glance. As a result he knew Maggie Lewis was the genuine article. No hidden agenda other than concealing her own weakness.

That stubborn pride was something he knew all about. Hadn't his father accused him of being too proud when Khalid had refused to live in indolent luxury? When instead he'd forged a life of hard work that brought its own rewards?

'At least you won't make the same mistake again.'

Solemn eyes met his before a shadow of a smile curved the corners of her mouth.

'Absolutely not! I'll *never* be that gullible again. I've learned my lesson.'

Intrigued, Khalid watched her rueful expression morph into one of determination. But even that was attractive…too attractive.

Her intelligence and character intrigued him as much as her vulnerability and her unvarnished beauty. She wasn't conventionally pretty, but there was something about the spare elegance of her features that drew the eye again and again. He wished she'd sat beside him at tonight's tedious dinner. Instead he'd been sandwiched between a yawning bore and a flirtatious airhead.

'He's a fool, whoever he is.'

'He?' She arched her eyebrows.

'The man tonight. The one who's caused you such grief.'

'How did you know there was a man?' She looked genuinely shocked.

He smiled at her naïvety. 'It's relationships between the sexes that cause most pain.'

'I can't imagine you having any such trouble,' she riposted instantly. A moment later her expression changed to one of dawning horror, as if she couldn't believe she'd just uttered the words. 'I'm sorry,' she whispered. 'I—'

'You'd be surprised,' he murmured as memories crowded in. 'Wealth is no guarantee of happiness.'

Maggie watched with a pang of regret as the vertical lines reformed at his brow and bracketed his mouth. For a little while there the grimness had lifted from Khalid's features. Now it was as if a storm cloud loomed, shadowing his face and blocking the hint of light she'd glimpsed.

She knew a crazy impulse to reach out and touch him, soothe away the pain she saw. But that wasn't an option. Instead she changed the subject.

'You're from Shajehar, aren't you?'

He nodded. 'I am.'

'Could you tell me about it? I've never travelled and it sounds so exotic.'

Dark eyes seared hers as if searching for an ulterior motive. Maggie shivered and rolled her collar higher against her throat. Perhaps she should go. It didn't matter if her clothes weren't dry, she'd been here long enough and that look made her nervous. But the raging storm and the long trip to her cold, empty house held no appeal.

'It's a country of contrasts and great beauty. Some parts are not unlike your Hunter Valley, though much is arid. There are wonderful riches if you care to look, and I'm not talking about oil revenue.' His expression told her he loved his homeland.

'The people are strong and proud of their traditions. But they're struggling now to meld their old ways with the best the modern world has to offer.' He paused, focused on her. 'You've never travelled overseas?'

'I've never been anywhere much.' At his curious look she

continued. 'I grew up on a small farm. Making ends meet was always a struggle. Travel was a luxury.'

'And when you left home?'

She ducked her head, watching her hands fold the thick fabric in her lap.

'I never left. I had plans to go to the city and study, but there was a drought and my father couldn't spare me.' He'd reminded her time and again that it was her duty to stand by him as he'd done his duty and kept her with him all those years. A pity his concept of duty didn't include even a skerrick of warmth or love.

'And now?'

'Now? I work here.'

'Helping your family?'

Maggie thought of the empty front bedroom in the old house, the echoing loneliness of the place she called home.

'There was only my father.' Maggie hadn't had any contact from her mother or sister since the day they'd left. 'He died a few months ago.'

'You must miss him.'

Must she? Miss the stern lectures, the disapproving attitude, the dour temperament?

'I... He wasn't an easy man to live with.' That had to be the understatement of the century. Nothing Maggie ever did had been good enough, even when her extra income had been all that kept the old farm afloat. 'He should have had a son. A daughter is a disappointment to a man like that.'

'I'm sorry, Maggie.' The words were filled with understanding. She darted a glance at Khalid. Was that compassion in his liquid dark eyes? 'Some of us aren't blessed with the best of parents.'

'You too?'

He paused, as if taken aback by the personal question.

'My father had no time for his family,' he said eventually. 'No time for children. He had...other interests.' Khalid's tone made it clear those interests weren't anything he approved of. 'He was an absentee parent, rarely home. And when he was, let's just say he had little patience with small boys.'

Reading between the lines, Maggie felt a sharp stab of fellow feeling, a sympathy for the suffering Khalid had skated over. For the stoic endurance not to collapse under the weight of a parent's cruel neglect.

'I'm sorry.' Her voice was husky. 'Little boys need a dad.'

'And so do little girls.'

To her horror, his ready sympathy cracked the brittle wall she'd built around her feelings. For years she'd struggled against the belief that she was unlovable, ever since her mum had rejected her, taking Cassie instead. Tonight her fears and pain had coalesced into an aching void of anguish that filled her very being. The force of it clogged her throat and fractured her breathing.

'Maggie.' Khalid must have seen the stricken expression on her face. He reached out and pulled her close, tucking her head into his shoulder. He rubbed her back with small, circular, soothing movements.

'You've done this before,' she murmured, trying to regain her composure and downplay her reaction to his touch. 'Do you have sisters?'

'No sisters.'

'A wife?'

She was dimly aware of his pause before he said, 'No wife.'

A heartbeat of silence and then he urged, 'Hold me, Maggie.'

She needed no second urging. Maggie slid her arms around him and burrowed close to his heat. She knew later she'd be horribly embarrassed but for now her need for comfort drove her beyond her usual diffidence.

His arms tightened around her and a shiver rippled through Maggie as his warmth seeped into her bones. The rock-solid strength of him, the tangible, living power of muscle and bone and sinew, were more real than anything else in the world. His unique spicy scent invaded her nostrils, making her nerves tingle into an awareness that had nothing to do with solace.

The scent, the feel, even the sound of him, the powerful throb of his heart beneath her ear, were all wondrous. She pressed her face to the fine silk of his shirt. Through the fabric his skin was hot, taut and inviting. She breathed deep, drawing in the heady aroma of warm, healthy male.

That was when she registered his quickening heartbeat, the changed tempo of his breathing. Tentatively she lifted a hand to splay over his chest.

The tiniest of tremors rippled across his skin. The hand palming her back ceased its movement and his other hand clamped down on her arm, as if to drag it away.

Thunder echoed in her ears as her pulse raced. Suddenly this innocent embrace had transformed into something charged with unspoken danger.

With excitement. And longing. It bubbled up inside her like a newfound spring—the need for more. The need for *him*. This was nothing like what she'd felt with Marcus. This was... elemental, as sudden as a thunderclap and just as unmistakable, even to someone of her limited experience.

Heat blossomed deep within as her breath caught, stilled by the stunning realisation of how much more she wanted from this man.

'It's time you moved.' His voice sounded stretched.

Heat flamed her cheeks. What was she thinking? He'd offered her comfort, not a sexual invitation. Just because she felt that sunburst of white-hot desire didn't mean it was reciprocated. Hadn't she learned anything tonight?

'Maggie, you need to sit up. You don't want to do something you'll regret later.'

She frowned. Something *she'd* regret?

'What do you mean?' she whispered at last.

Strong hands pried her away, gently pushing her back to her corner of the sofa. Ebony eyes met hers. His face was grim, his mouth a tight line.

'You're upset. You're not yourself. It's time to end this. You don't want to play with fire.'

'Fire?' She wasn't normally obtuse, but surely he didn't mean what she thought he meant. Was it even remotely possible that he felt it too? The sudden overwhelming need for intimacy that ousted everything else? The consuming hunger? A need for *her*, for plain, no-frills Maggie Lewis?

His gaze narrowed, flicking down to her mouth, and lower to the V-neck of the robe she wore. Flames licked her skin beneath his trailing gaze and tension coiled tight in her belly as her breathing shortened.

'I'm a man, Maggie. If we don't stop now it won't be comfort I'll be giving you. It will be something much more intimate.'

The words echoed on and on in the silence between them. They should have shocked her, made her draw back. But instead the blatant weight of sensuality in his bald statement had the opposite effect. Excitement tingled down her spine and drew her stomach muscles tight.

Maggie strove to be sensible, careful, reserved, all the things she'd been before tonight.

But something vital had changed. Now, for the first time, she knew what it was to want a man. *Really* want, with every fibre of her body. It was an urgent, unstoppable force. A compulsion shuddering through her very bones.

She had two choices. She could pretend this wasn't real. Shrug on her usual self-effacing persona and try to hide from this surge of powerful desire. Or she could welcome it; give in to the strongest need she'd ever felt.

She could be bold or she could be sensible.

She'd spent a lifetime being sensible and self-sacrificing. Where had that got her?

'And you don't want to do that?'

She didn't recognise her hoarse voice. Excitement and anxiety closed her throat. She couldn't believe she'd just invited another rebuff, but the new sensations heating her blood were too compelling to ignore. She had to know.

Hooded eyes surveyed her and she felt the distance grow between them. He was going to reject her. Something dimmed inside her.

Finally he spoke. 'I shouldn't.' He raised his hand and thrust it back through his hair in a jerky gesture. 'I shouldn't but…yes, God help me, I want to.'

CHAPTER THREE

HE COULDN'T. He mustn't.

This woman was exhausted, not thinking clearly. He mustn't take advantage, no matter that his need for her was visceral, all-consuming. She deserved his protection.

Her eyes glowed a shimmering green-gold. She looked pale but beautiful, her fine-boned features pure, alluring and incredibly sexy with that hopeful pout.

'You're hurt. This is your pain speaking.' Khalid forced the words out. 'But this isn't the answer. You want someone who can give you more. More than a few snatched hours.'

More than a man who could only promise physical pleasure. Who had given up on emotional commitment years before.

For one absurd moment he felt a piercing jealousy for the man who'd one day give Maggie Lewis everything she wanted.

Her chin tilted fractionally in a way that spoke of pride and pain together.

'What if I said a few snatched hours are exactly what I want? That I'm not in the market for anything more? Not any longer?'

Tension held Khalid rigid as desire spiralled and his groin tightened. Each muscle was rock-hard at the effort of remaining still when he wanted to lean over and imprison her beneath his hungry body.

Desire he understood. He had a healthy male appreciation

of a sexy woman. But this craving was something else entirely. It shook him to the core. Unbelievably this felt far more significant than the simple sexual urge he'd assuaged through the recent years with beautiful, willing women.

This felt...different. More real, more vital than anything he'd experienced in years.

A shadowed vision of velvet-soft brown eyes filled his mind and pain lanced his chest.

'No. I can't.' He forced the words out over a constricting throat.

'Yes, of course.' Her whisper drew his sensitised flesh to prickling alert. 'I understand.'

Khalid drew a shuddering breath. He'd done the right thing, the honourable thing. Now he just had to—

The sight of her bowed head, her white teeth cutting deep into her bottom lip, brought him up short.

'Thank you for helping me tonight,' she said stiffly, looking away. 'I'm sorry I embarrassed you with my...with my...' She shook her head and soft hair the colour of toffee swirled round her neck, catching the light.

'I apologise,' she murmured, wrapping her arms around herself. 'You must have women coming on to you all the time.'

Apologise?

Her profile was taut, her lips pinched. His chest hollowed as he realised he'd caused her more distress. Instinct overcame caution as he cupped her chin in his hand and turned her face around. She resisted, even grabbed his wrist as if to tug his arm away.

'You don't owe me an apology.'

Bright eyes met his, startled and disbelieving. He wished the texture of her soft skin weren't so enticing.

Khalid hoped fate would repay him one day for his superhuman restraint. It was killing him by degrees, inhaling her tantalising scent, sexier than any bottled fragrance. The feel of her, the sight of her, seduced him, more real than any shadowy memories of the past. That scared him, yet he ached to learn the taste of her.

She reared back, away from his touch. Her chest rose and fell rapidly beneath the oversized robe.

'I understand.' She spoke too quickly, her words tripping over each other. 'It's all right.'

But it wasn't. She thought he lied about wanting her. Could she really be so blind? What had happened tonight to make her so unsure of her attractiveness?

'I think I should leave.' Her voice wobbled on the last word. Automatically she angled her chin higher as if to counteract any sign of weakness.

She was a fighter, this woman who played havoc with his good intentions, who'd got under his skin from the moment he'd seen her. Who had to be one of the most alluring women he'd ever met. Even without make-up, drenched and shivering in her underwear, she'd exerted a terrible fascination.

The hot tide rose in him, welling and cresting, and his resolve crumbled, his caution disintegrated.

One kiss. He'd permit himself a single kiss to alleviate the compulsive need to touch her again. To reassure her that she *was* desirable.

'Maggie.' Once more he lifted her chin, this time bending close. Her eyes widened, her mouth slackened just a little as she realised what he intended. Perfect.

Her lips trembled beneath his and he wrapped his arms around her, sweeping her close. The brush of her slender, feminine form and her fresh, sweet taste on his tongue sent a roaring wave of need juddering through him. Khalid breathed deep, summoning control. He had to concentrate, to keep this a gentle, exploratory kiss.

The feel of her lips shaping to his and the sound of her soft sigh were poignant. She fitted his arms as if made for him. It was as perfect as any lover's kiss he'd known.

He reeled as the discovery slammed into his astonished brain.

Her tongue slid tentatively against his as he entered her mouth and a dart of pure pleasure shafted through him.

Just another minute…

Maggie clung to his shoulders as the world spun and she closed her eyes, dizzy with delight. The feelings he evoked with the touch of his mouth and his arms holding her close swept her into a new world.

She felt desire, daring, a thrill of excitement as his tongue stroked her mouth. Shivers ran down her spine, along her arms where the skin pulled tight and down to her nipples. She gasped as he delved deeper.

Their hearts pulsed in unison, their mouths fused as need exploded. She clamped her hands desperately to the back of his skull, pulling herself higher, closer.

Still, it wasn't enough.

Her need for him was a twisting, hungry sensation in the pit of her stomach, and lower, where a curious ache filled her. Maggie squirmed, trying to ease the hollow feeling deep within.

Recklessly she kissed him back, the fever in her blood urging her on. For now, for tonight, this was what she craved, the sweet headiness of shared passion. All Khalid's magnificent power concentrated on her.

When he cupped her breast she gasped against his mouth, unprepared for the electric charge his touch evoked. Blue-white fire flickered behind her eyelids as he brushed his thumb over her nipple. Incendiary sparks exploded through her, drawing her body tight and expectant.

Maggie pressed forward into his hand and was rewarded as he firmed his hold. She arched her back in a spasm of pleasure. Yes!

'Please,' she mouthed, not even knowing what it was she pleaded for.

Devastation hit when he removed his hand, but a moment later he slipped it into the neckline of her robe. Her skin contracted, sensitised to his touch. His hand closed again around her breast, only this time there was nothing between him and her. No barrier. The feeling of him slowly massaging, then gently squeezing her there was indescribable. Perfect.

She sagged back against his embracing arm, breaking their devastating kiss as she gulped oxygen into her air-starved lungs. She gazed up at him.

Eyes like glittering dark pools shone down at her, unreadable. His shoulders rose and fell as he breathed quick and deep. His heavy-lidded eyelids spoke of passion, tightly leashed. So powerfully controlled.

Would he go now? Would he slide his hand away? Could he possibly leave her alone and so desperately wanting?

She couldn't bear it. He'd given her a taste of something special, miraculous, something only he could give. And she wanted more. Was it so bad to seek, just this once, the intimate pleasure she'd never had?

Maggie covered his hand with her own, pressing into his hold. His fingers tightened and delicious ripples spread through her.

'Please, Khalid.' She knew what she asked this time. She wanted him to show her more, let her experience the intimate joy of truly being with a man.

His face looked grim, the flickering firelight emphasising the sharp cut of his cheekbones, the hard, aristocratic line of his nose and his set jaw.

He was going to do it, she realised. He was going to leave her. Pride warred with need. Already tonight she'd cast aside any pretence of dignity.

Wordlessly she pulled the other side of the robe open to reveal her bare breast.

Cool air shivered across her skin.

Her heart pounded fast in trepidation and anticipation. She watched the muscles work in his throat as he swallowed. Then his chest expanded on a mighty breath.

She waited, trembling, but his next move was to slip his hand away.

Maggie knew defeat then. He didn't like what he saw. Why was she surprised? She'd always known she wasn't feminine enough with her underdeveloped curves. She dragged the robe back, covering herself, even though it was too late for modesty.

The touch of his hands made her jump. Before she could gather her wits she was hauled off the couch and up into steel-hard arms. His eyes were molten hot as they clashed with hers.

'Are you sure you want this?' His voice was a low burr that reverberated deep in that hollow place within her.

She nodded, her mouth too dry to speak as excitement effervesced in her bloodstream. There was silence but for the crackle of the fire. Maggie held her breath, waiting.

'Then so be it.'

He turned so fast the room blurred. A moment later they were in a massive, shadowed bedroom. Maggie had an impression of sumptuous furnishings, of a vast royal-blue and gold bedspread, before he ripped the covers back in a single ruthless tug and tumbled her down onto the sheets.

Their eyes met and held and her blood pumped harder, faster. It was a thunderous buzz in her ears as his hands went to his shirt and he tugged it off, not bothering with buttons. Seconds later the rest of his clothing dropped to the floor.

He stood before her, magnificent and more beautiful than anything she'd seen in her life. The warm glow of the bedroom fire gilded his skin and cast shadows across his body. Each plane and curved muscle was thrown into relief. He was long-limbed, strong and virile. She'd never imagined a man could look so potent, so perfect.

Maggie pushed back a moment's doubt, wondering if she should tell him she was a virgin. He wouldn't have taken seriously her crack about being untouched.

But she didn't want him having second thoughts now. A man such as this must have had many lovers. Would he be disappointed? Maggie quashed the worry as soon as it entered her brain.

For this one night she'd live for the moment, thrust caution aside and take what life had to offer.

Heat washed her as he reached into a bedside drawer to retrieve a foil packet and put it on the table.

She was grateful he'd thought of protection, but somehow this reminder of real-world responsibility made her feel awkward and nervous.

'You have too many clothes on.' His words short-circuited her thoughts. The sound of his voice drew her skin tight over her bones. Then his hands were on her, drawing the belt from her robe, slowly opening it, laying the sides wide so she lay virtually naked. He stood there, not saying a word as his gaze travelled the length of her body. She had time to feel anxious again, wondering what he thought of it.

He drew in a deep breath and Maggie watched, mesmerised, the movement of muscle and tendon tightening across his torso. He had the superb body of an athlete.

Then there was no chance for further thought as he bent and stripped the robe away, flinging it to the floor. A moment later he was crowding her back on the bed. His body was as hot as a furnace. Everywhere they touched she registered unfamiliar, exciting sensations. The brush of wiry hair as his legs tangled with hers. The impossibly erotic slide of his chest against her heated skin; hard-packed muscle and a drift of silky hair against her own sensitised breasts. And, lower, his heavy erection on her thigh.

Her breath shuddered as sensory overload hit.

But there was more to come. He lowered his head to her breast and ecstasy consumed her.

'Khalid!' Her hoarse cry was barely audible as she fought to catch her breath. The sensations coursing through her as he suckled, at first gently, then hard, stiffened her body in shocked delight. Then his hand was on her other breast, circling and teasing. She wondered if it was possible to die from pleasure. His body heat against hers was exquisitely exciting.

Her fingers speared through his thick hair, holding him close. Liquid heat throbbed through her bloodstream and pooled between her legs. An urgent longing filled her. She wanted him. Now.

But Khalid was in no hurry.

'Patience, little one.' He turned his attention to discovering her body with a single-minded intensity that made her head spin and her blood sing.

From her shoulder to her fingertips, from the sensitive place just behind her ear to her collarbone and her breasts, he took his time caressing, kissing, learning her. Arousing her. She sighed as he moved lower, to her navel, her hipbone, her thigh, even the back of her knee.

Pleasure rippled through her as sensation after sensation bombarded her. She grew alternately limp and stiff with excitement at his touch. The one constant was the ever-building need that grew stronger by the minute. Soon it was a throbbing ache.

Hours might have passed by the time he paused to reach out a hand to the bedside table. Then he was back, his hard hands tender, his breath hot on her sensitive inner thighs and higher, on the place where the heat scorched brightest and hottest.

She cried out as he caressed her there, at the very apex of her need, and she almost jolted off the bed as jagged lightning shot through.

She was burning up; she couldn't breathe. Her pounding heart must surely suffocate her.

'Khalid.' Her fingers dug into his shoulders as she tried to drag him higher. Her legs twisted wide as instinctively she offered herself.

There was no doubt in her mind now. This was right. *He* was right. It was almost as if he was the one she'd been waiting for all this time.

The burgeoning realisation fractured into nothingness as he covered her body with his and she ceased to think.

He was heat and power, hard muscle and surprisingly silky skin. Maggie slipped her hands around his neck, her breath faltering as her breasts rubbed his chest.

Dark, fathomless eyes held hers and amidst the maelstrom of desire she felt...safe.

She hung on tight as he propped himself up on one arm and she felt the muscles in his shoulders ripple. His other hand moved down to touch her between her legs. His fingers glided through slick folds, over the throbbing nub and inexorably lower. Wildfire blazed in her bloodstream at his touch. Her body convulsed as he pushed inwards and her breath tore away.

For a long quivering moment she waited, eyes wide, fingers clenching tight in his hair as her body tugged at him. She saw his pulse jerk heavily in his throat and felt the throb of his erection against her.

She shifted against him, not sure how to proceed but knowing she'd die if he stopped now.

Clumsily she unwound an arm from around his neck and slid it down till her fingers curled around him. He came to life at her touch, pushing into her palm: hot, heavy and powerfully strong. Tentatively she squeezed.

A guttural rumble of Arabic near her ear might have been encouragement or an oath.

'Stop!'

Instantly she loosened her hold.

Khalid's lips were drawn back in a grimace of pain. Or pleasure? His eyes glittered febrile-bright as he stared down at her.

Then he moved and there were no more doubts. He braced himself over her as his palm spread her thighs wider. Her legs shook as she complied. He nudged at her entrance and instinctively she rose up to meet him.

He dipped his head to her neck, kissing and grazing her

tender skin with his teeth as he pushed in. The movement was smooth, easy and impossibly long. Maggie experienced a strange sensation of fullness, of stretching, of weight and heat. There was discomfort at first, but when he stopped she couldn't believe the feeling of oneness.

Khalid raised his head, a pinch of a frown marking the centre of his brow. He stared down at her through narrowed eyes for a long moment. Then raised a hand to her cheek in the gentlest of caresses. To her amazement Maggie registered a tiny tremor in his touch.

She turned her face into his palm, revelling in the slide of his callused fingers against her cheek.

'You are a treasure. So generous,' he murmured in a deep husky voice that curled her insides.

His mouth took hers in a sensuous kiss. His body moved away, then slid back, again and again in an easy rhythm that set incendiary sparks flying through her body. Frantically she hugged him, giving him back kiss for desperate kiss as the tension coiled tighter and tighter inside her.

Then the fire they'd built consumed her in a flare of white-hot light and the world exploded around her, blotting out everything but the perfection of that single climactic moment that went on and on and on.

It was dark when Maggie woke. Time for her early start in the stables. Yet she didn't stir. She felt lethargic, yet energised. She tingled with effervescent energy as if her bloodstream ran with champagne.

Her lips curved as she snuggled down on her pillow, enjoying the remarkable sense of well-being that filled her. She felt like a different woman. Not plain old Maggie Lewis. Then she registered the heat behind her. The living heat of another body.

Khalid.

Memory crashed upon her in a bitter-sweet tide.

She thought of last night, of Khalid's passion and the way he'd made her feel...beautiful. She'd never been given such a gift before. She hugged the memory tight to herself.

When he'd made love to her she'd even, for a moment, believed herself to be a desirable woman.

The tentative curve of her lips faded. Her mouth flattened into a grim line. Her—desirable? No, she couldn't fool herself like that. She was strong enough to face the truth.

Khalid had made love to her because she'd thrown herself at him. She'd seen the pity in his eyes. She'd read his initial unwillingness. She'd played on his sympathy and he'd read her desperation.

It didn't matter that she'd needed him so badly she'd felt she might shatter with the force of her feelings. Or that their love-making had been the most wonderful experience in all her twenty-three years.

Last night she'd told herself she should grab what she wanted. Anger had welled at Marcus's duplicity, at the dull, demanding life she'd accepted for so long, at the hurt she'd endured. She'd wanted for one night the powerful pleasure she'd known instinctively Khalid could give her.

He'd probably spent the encounter thinking of some voluptuous beauty, not the awkward emotional woman in his arms.

Mortified, Maggie felt her face burn.

She was strong, a survivor. But did she have the nerve to face him this morning? She imagined him trying to stifle his distaste.

Maggie darted a furtive look over her shoulder. He lay asleep. Even in the pre-dawn gloom the set of his shoulders and deep chest above white sheets snared her gaze. Heat built inside her. That needy ache was back again.

No! She buried her face in her pillow, only to inhale the faint spicy scent that lingered there. The evocative scent of Khalid's skin. Her resolve splintered. The temptation to stay was so strong.

But Maggie was done with fantasy. Last night had been a wonderful, once-in-a-lifetime experience, but it couldn't lead anywhere. Better to let Khalid wake alone. He deserved that. He'd be relieved to find she wasn't clinging to him still.

Slowly, her heart heavy, she pulled back the covers and slipped noiselessly from the bed.

Khalid woke at dawn. His recall of last night was instantaneous, evidenced by his early-morning erection. Despite the startling perfection of sex with Maggie Lewis it had been a frustrating night. Once was rarely enough for Khalid and last night his climax, despite its rare intensity, had barely scratched the surface of his need. He'd itched for more.

Only the knowledge that, incredibly, he was her first lover had restrained him from sating himself in her slim, sexy body again and again.

A powerful shudder ran through him.

Her first. The knowledge stirred a deeply primitive satisfaction in his belly. He didn't deflower virgins. He sought pleasure with women who were worldly, experienced and unlikely to cling. Women who knew he no longer had a heart to bestow even on the most generous lover.

Yet here he was, rampant with sexual hunger for his next taste of Maggie.

Last night's shock at her inexperience had worn off. So too had his reservations, that hint of guilt that he'd taken advantage of her vulnerability. She'd wanted him. Had eagerly welcomed him. Then afterwards had curled into him with the trusting innocence of a kitten. No, there could be no regrets.

The liaison had been unlooked-for, but now it had begun he knew no qualms about pursuing it further. He was a generous lover and she would have no regrets. He'd change his flights to extend his stay. But first… He rolled over, seeking the warm, welcoming embrace of his new lover.

The bed was empty.

He swiped his arm over the sheets. There was barely a trace of her warmth. A single movement propelled him out of bed, striding across the room. She wasn't in the bathroom. Her clothes had disappeared.

Khalid's puzzled frown accelerated into a scowl.

She'd left him without as much as a word? As if he was some sordid secret to be ashamed of! He sucked in a deep breath and willed his clenched hands to relax. But nothing could stem the surge of annoyance, of…outrage.

Never had a woman walked out on him. His pride rebelled at the very idea. Usually he was the one distancing himself from importunate lovers.

He swung round, scanning the room. No note. No explanation. Annoyance and frustration warred with curiosity. What had sent her hurtling out of bed at that ungodly hour? Fear? Guilt?

For a moment he pictured her racing off to sell her kiss-and-tell story to some slimy tabloid. The press was insatiably hungry for stories about him.

But…could he have been so wrong about her? Instinct told him not, told him she was exactly what she'd seemed last night. But he'd better make sure.

The buzz of his mobile phone caught his attention, interrupting his unwanted doubts. One glance at the caller ID had him connecting the call and sinking into a chair.

Ten minutes later he ended the call and stared across the shadowy room, his eyes fixed on a distant place.

Khalid's world had changed in those few minutes.

Faruq was dead. Khalid was Sheikh of Shajehar.

He drew a slow breath, thinking of the half-brother he'd barely known. There'd been no love between them, but regret pierced him at that life cut short.

After a while he rolled his shoulders and stood. His people needed him. He'd return immediately. He paused, his gaze settling on the wide, rumpled bed. He had no time to look for

Maggie Lewis now. Yet there was unfinished business between them.

The situation was easily remedied. He'd have her located and brought to Shajehar. His lips curled in a faint smile.

It would be his pleasure to renew their acquaintance.

CHAPTER FOUR

'COME on, Tally. Let's get this show on the road.'

Late-morning sun beat down on Maggie through her long-sleeved cotton shirt as she led Tallawanta's Pride to the ring. The dry heat reminded her of an Aussie summer and the smell of horse, hay and sawdust was comfortably familiar.

Yet everything else was different in Shajehar. The stables were infinitely more luxurious than in Australia. The sheikh obviously lavished a fortune on his horses.

Pity he didn't give as much attention to his people. In the days since she'd flown in, accompanying the Tallawanta horses, she'd seen the stark divide between rich and poor. Extravagant modern complexes beside slums.

'Almost there, Tally,' she whispered as the mare caught an unfamiliar scent and shuddered to a halt. The flight to the Middle East had been a long one for the horses. Only now, after lengthy veterinary checks, were they being paraded for the sheikh's approval.

Not that he'd deigned to come. Always the cushioned seat at the centre of the ringside stand, the gilt-covered chair set aside for the sheikh, had been empty.

She tensed as they entered the ring, scanning the crowd for the imposing figure of the man who kept her awake each night.

Khalid. The thought of him sent excitement skimming down her spine, though it was a month since they'd been together.

She hadn't seen him since the morning after they'd made love. She'd thrown herself into her work, hoping to erase the memory of her behaviour that night. But nothing could blank the recollection of Khalid holding her, loving her. No matter how she berated herself, she couldn't prevent the fillip of delight inside when she remembered.

She'd spent the next day fearful he'd visit the stables. She'd been on tenterhooks, anxious that she might come face to face with the man who'd made her discover a new Maggie. A needy, sensuous, wanton woman who responded to his touch with a total lack of control.

Yet when she'd overheard someone mention the stud's VIP guest had changed his plans and left that morning, it hadn't been relief she'd felt. It had been disappointment.

A small foolish part of her had hoped their passionate encounter had meant something to him. That he'd want to see her again. But she'd been an object of pity, nothing more.

Maggie notched her chin up as she led the mare around the ring. Khalid was probably on the other side of the world with some beautiful sophisticate in tow.

Sunlight glinted to her left and movement caught her eye— new arrivals taking their seats in the stand.

Maggie faltered as she caught a glimpse of the man at the centre of the newcomers. Tall, lean and dressed in concealing robes. But the stark white fabric couldn't hide a pair of spectacular shoulders, a physique that made him top his companions by a head.

It couldn't be.

He was obscured by a bowing usher yet Maggie was sure she'd seen a familiar profile: spare, powerful and unmistakable. Her stomach churned and fire fizzed through her bloodstream.

Khalid.

If it was him, what then? Would he acknowledge her or pretend they were strangers?

Maggie bit her lip. Would he remember her? He was a

man with a wealth of sensual experience. No doubt there were plenty of women—beautiful and glamorous—who'd captivated his attention for more than a couple of hours.

No, he'd remember that night for a while at least. It *had* been out of the ordinary—making love to a gawky, bedraggled wreck of a woman.

A shout and a loud whinny from the entry tunnel snapped her out of her reverie. She clung to the lead-rein as Tally sidled abruptly towards her. Tally plunged and it took all Maggie's strength to hold the spooked mare. Her arms felt as if they were being ripped out of their sockets. But she knew her job and her horse, and soon had it under control.

The same couldn't be said for Tallawanta Diva. Maggie caught a flash of black as the horse thundered into the ring, kicking up sand and sawdust, its head tossing wildly.

Damn it. She'd counselled against giving Diva to a new, untried groom. Diva was too skittish and unsettled and far too mettlesome for inexperienced hands. But the stable manager had insisted. Maggie wished it could be the stable manager who caught the fractious horse.

Swiftly she turned towards the ringside seating and thrust Tally's lead-rein into the hands of the local trainer who'd worked with the horses. His startled eyes met hers, then she was spinning away, striding to where the other horse ran loose.

The new groom picked himself up, looking stiff and wary. Meanwhile Diva showed every symptom of a highly strung beast who was out of routine, out of familiar surroundings and working herself into a frenzy. Maggie saw the whites of her eyes as she tossed her head and lashed out with her hindquarters at a silk banner waving on the edge of the ring. She skittered sideways at a ripple of movement in the stands as spectators rose, eager to watch.

Maggie didn't take her eyes off her for a second. She knew only too well the power of the animal. None of the grooms turned their back on this horse. Slowly she approached, keeping her voice low and soothing.

Diva listened, ears flicking back and forth at Maggie's familiar tone, but still sidling nervously, muscles twitching and head jerking at each movement in the encircling stands. Every so often she'd swing round to lash out at a shadow or at the banner snapping in the breeze.

A deep, authoritative voice called out something short and sharp in Arabic, then, thankfully, the spectators subsided in their seats. Thank goodness someone in the audience had had the sense to see the horse was spooked by the rippling movement of so many long robes.

At last Maggie was close enough. Keeping eye contact, talking all the while, she stepped forward, reaching for the lead-rein. Her fingers touched leather. She almost had it.

Suddenly the horse reared, spun round and backed towards the ringside. Maggie had an instant's grace to extricate herself from the gap between horse and stand. She almost made it. Then she was crammed back against the wooden structure and pain slammed into her.

A moment later Diva danced sideways and Maggie snatched the chance to brace herself, head bent and hands on knees, gasping in air. Then she straightened and turned to the horse. There was pin-drop silence in the ring.

Maggie circled, hand raised to grab the lead-rein. Then she discovered the job had already been done. Someone stood at Diva's head, holding her steady.

Through the smells of sawdust and horse Maggie caught another scent. Sandalwood and warm, male skin. She stopped dead. Diva moved and suddenly Maggie caught sight of the man who'd vaulted into the ring to capture the mare.

'Khalid!'

Maggie's heart revved and her throat closed on an instantaneous burst of pleasure. He looked so good.

His expression was hard, his mouth a taut straight line

bracketed by grim slashes. His ebony-dark eyes had narrowed, his nostrils flared as if he needed extra oxygen. Or as if he clamped down on anger.

He looked all male in a way that sent spurts of excitement racing through her. With his face framed by a pristine head-cloth that emphasised his dark tan, he looked the epitome of some exotic fantasy.

He held the mare with the easy competence of an experienced horseman. Already Diva was calming.

In the bright light of the open air Khalid was even more arresting than she remembered. Heat blazed deep inside as her mind strayed to the memory of him naked, his superb body gilded by flickering firelight.

'Maggie.' His tone was abrupt. 'You're on your feet? You need to sit and get your breath back.' Clearly he wasn't disturbed by memories of their night together. He was anchored firmly in the here and now. Embarrassment washed her in a hot tide and she drew herself up taller.

'I'm OK.' The response was automatic.

Dark eyes held hers while her pulse thumped in her throat. What was he thinking? Was he remembering?

'That remains to be seen.' He turned and gestured and the head groom appeared. Khalid said something in Arabic and the groom nodded before leading Diva away.

'I'm perfectly capable of…' Maggie's voice died as Khalid lifted warm hands to her face, his touch like a benediction on her skin. Slowly he dragged long fingers down her throat and across her shoulders.

Sensations sparked from his touch and rippled out across her skin. Convulsively she swallowed.

His touch was light. The brush of his fingers across her skin reignited sensations she'd discovered for the first time weeks ago. When he'd caressed her, aroused her.

'No! I'm fine.' She tried to jerk out of his grasp but his grip firmed on her upper arms.

Had he stepped closer? His body heat seared through the cotton of her shirt and his eyes were so close she felt she could lose herself in their glittering depths.

'We need to make sure.' His tone was adamant as he cast an eye over her dusty clothes.

Maggie, brought up on her father's maxim of 'no tears, no complaints, just get up and get on with it', couldn't believe how easily she subsided in the face of Khalid's determination. Obviously he was a man used to issuing orders and receiving unquestioning obedience.

She could barely believe he was here.

'Do you make a habit of rescuing strange women?' Her voice was husky.

His mouth quirked up briefly in what might have been a smile. Or a grimace. 'You're my first.' He met her gaze then. The intensity of his look dried her throat instantly. No more flippant remarks.

For a moment Maggie was back in Australia, in bed. Khalid leaned over her, his glorious naked body propped above her, his eyes warm with the promise of delight. Desire swirled like hot treacle in her abdomen.

Then she registered a buzz of sound. Belatedly she re-membered they weren't alone. This time when she tried to step away he didn't prevent her. His hands dropped to his sides. For an absurd moment she felt…bereft.

Maggie turned and saw, beyond him, a cluster of strang-ers watching with concern and open curiosity. Blood rushed to her cheeks.

'What were you doing here?' she whispered. It was easier to focus on him than the encircling onlookers.

His brows rose. 'Viewing the horses.'

Of course. His presence had nothing to do with her. Hadn't she already guessed he'd probably prefer to be anywhere else than with her? At Tallawanta he'd accepted her departure easily, choosing to leave the estate without trying to contact her.

He met her eyes, his expression unreadable. 'We'll have a doctor examine you.'

'No, I'm OK.' She cast a look around the ring but the horses had disappeared. 'I'm needed in the stables.'

'Nevertheless, it would be sensible.'

'But—'

'Especially since you are a visitor here.' His voice brooked no argument. 'We take our responsibilities to our guests very seriously. You need to be fit to do your job.'

'Sire.' A man stepped forward from the group around them. 'The doctor is here as requested.'

Maggie frowned. *Sire?*

'I don't need a doctor!' She was horrified at the fuss they were making. 'Look, this is overkill.'

'Let him do his job,' Khalid said in a low voice that only she could hear. 'Unless you'd prefer to make a scene?'

The tilt of one sleek eyebrow dared her to argue. She shook her head. If submitting to a medical check meant she could escape these curious eyes, she'd do it.

'Good. Sensible woman.'

Watching Khalid, Maggie was struck by the knowledge that, for all they'd shared, he was a stranger. In a long robe that emphasised the lean power of his tall frame and a *keffiyeh* hiding his dark hair, he looked exotically foreign. His expression was unreadable but his stance was commanding. She noticed that the other spectators, for all their curiosity, kept back a few paces.

Then the doctor was there, distracting her thoughts. He bowed to Khalid before checking for injuries. Then he announced that she should accompany him. Good. The sooner she escaped this crowd, the better. She was mortified at this fuss. And at the impossible yearning she felt still for Khalid's touch, his tenderness.

If fate was kind, she wouldn't see him again. Then she

could pretend her reaction to him was due to shock and not, as she feared, something far stronger.

Khalid paused before the door to the first-aid room, glad he'd finally shaken his entourage. He hadn't missed the speculative glances at the ring. They were used to Faruq, who had been too lazy and self-indulgent to bestir himself for anyone else, much less an employee. He'd never have personally rescued a groom from the trampling kicks of a frightened horse.

Khalid could imagine the whispers circulating about him and the Australian stable hand. The graceful, courageous, *female* stable hand.

He'd already made a name for himself as an unconventional ruler, more serious and hardworking than either his father or half-brother. Now the courtiers would wonder if at last he exhibited a family weakness for beautiful women. Whether the slim girl with the wide eyes and luscious mouth had captured his fancy.

Let them speculate. If he'd waited to intervene…

Khalid's blood had run cold, seeing her in danger. He'd ordered the spectators to sit, to give her a chance to quieten the thoroughbred. She'd almost done it too. She'd shown no fear or doubt, just a single-minded intent and a reckless disregard for her own safety that had filled him with admiration even as it had chilled him.

He reached for the door, deliberately taking his time.

Four weeks since he'd been with this woman. Yet the impact of her in the flesh was more devastating than he'd expected. He'd told himself his memory was faulty. That he'd imagined that intense sensual spark between them.

Perhaps this compelling sense of unfinished business, this acute physical hunger, stemmed from the fact that Maggie Lewis had, uniquely among women, walked away from him.

Khalid Bin Shareef was not a man used to being denied.

For all his modern education, his forebears had been arrogant and strong leaders, who took what they wanted.

His blood sizzled in anticipation as he rapped on the door, paused and then pushed it open.

She sat primly in an upright chair. Why didn't it surprise him that she wasn't lying down after what must have been a frightening experience?

Her light toffee hair fell around her shoulders. She looked dirty, dishevelled and ridiculously alluring. Perhaps because he could so easily picture the creamy smooth skin and pert pink nipples beneath her shirt.

He didn't want to remember. It would have been so much easier if he could look at her again and feel nothing. But even that first glance at her in the ring, her profile clear and proud, her body supple and tempting, had brought his libido roaring into life, making him pause to watch before taking his seat in the centre of the stand.

A knot of desire tightened his groin as he saw her mouth slacken in surprise. He recalled her soft, astonished gasp of pleasure as he'd brought her to climax. The sound of it, the remembrance of her innocent temptation, had haunted his nights ever since.

'What are you doing here?'

Maggie could have bitten her tongue as soon as the words were out. She sounded waspish.

Last time they'd met she'd been a wreck. Was she destined always to be at a disadvantage with him? She was grimy and tired and the doctor's continued absence was making her jittery. She sat straighter, watching Khalid cross the room with his long, easy stride.

'Hello, Maggie. It's a pleasure to see you too.' There wasn't a hint of reproach in his voice, but he looked grim. She curled her fingers tight round the edge of the chair.

'Hello, Khalid.' Just the sound of his name on her lips sent excitement twisting inside her. She notched up her chin, as if to repudiate the reaction.

'What was the doctor's verdict?'

She shrugged. 'I'm fine. I'll be back to the stables soon.' At Khalid's querying look she added, 'The doctor is just running a couple of tests.'

When she'd mentioned that she'd felt a little light-headed lately the doctor had kept her longer. But surely that odd sensation had been due to the bustle and excitement of her first overseas trip. Maggie had spent the last weeks so busy she'd been more exhausted than she could ever remember.

'You walked out of the lodge without a word,' Khalid said abruptly. 'Why?'

Maggie stared at him, horrified at the change of subject, and wondering where to start. She had nothing in common with this man who was clearly a VIP. A man of power and wealth who'd taken pity on her when she'd hit rock-bottom. That night was best forgotten.

She braced her shoulders, stiffening her spine as she met his glittering eyes head-on.

'We had nothing to discuss.'

She didn't want him thinking she was some clinging vine, shown pity once and ever after seeking what she patently couldn't have. Pride came to her rescue and kept her gaze steady.

'Not even the fact that you were a virgin before you took me into your body?'

Her gasp was loud in the silent room.

'How did you know?' she blurted out, then silently cursed herself. No doubt her clumsy embraces had been eloquent testimony to her lack of experience. She didn't need him to spell it out for her.

He took a single pace towards her. That was close enough for her to feel the sizzle of his presence. The air between them almost zapped and crackled.

'You were untried. Your body told me.'

Maggie bit her lip as blood rushed to her cheeks. At least he'd spared her comparisons with his other lovers.

'So?' The single syllable sounded belligerent. Better that than pathetic.

'Don't you think I wanted to know you were all right?'

'Of course I was all right! It was just sex, after all.' The blush intensified as the words spilled out of her mouth. Inside she cringed.

'Just sex.' His lips pursed and his eyes narrowed as if he were seeing her for the first time, assessing her and finding her wanting. He shook his head. 'We both know it was far more than that, Maggie. How old are you?'

The question threw her off balance and she answered automatically.

'Twenty-three. Why?'

'Twenty-three and a virgin.' His brows tilted up as if in surprise. 'That's not so common these days.'

Of course, he was an expert on the matter! Maggie opened her mouth to say so, then snapped it shut as she realised he probably had far more knowledge of the subject than she did. With his tantalising good looks and that subtle air of command, he'd cut a swathe through women wherever he went.

His lips twisted up in a brief smile that sent a tingle of shocking pleasure through her. There was an edgy, unsettled sensation deep in her pelvis, a hollow ache she'd never known before the night they'd first met. And when he looked at her, his eyes hooded and secretive, her nipples tightened and puckered. She lifted one hand to grasp her other arm, trying to look nonchalant as she hid her pebbling nipples from his view.

'You had been saving yourself,' he murmured in a tone so deep it made her skin tingle.

She shrugged. 'Even if I was, it didn't matter. The man I'd thought was the one wasn't what I'd believed him to be.'

Her night with Khalid had achieved one thing at least: it

had shown her just how little Marcus had really meant to her. She'd been in love with the idea of love. Her night of intimacy with Khalid had blasted the illusion apart with a white-hot surge of power and the old, naïve Maggie had gone. Now she was stronger by far, unencumbered by stupid fantasies.

'You're not still in love with him?'

She shook her head and turned to stare out the window at the cloudless sky. 'No. I don't think I ever was.'

The sound of the door opening made her swing her head around. Thank goodness. The doctor. At least now the personal questions would stop. And with the doctor here she wouldn't be tempted to meet Khalid's liquid dark eyes again. Each time she did her stomach went into free fall.

'Sire.' The doctor stopped abruptly just inside the room. 'Shall I come back later?'

'No, no.' Khalid waved him forward. 'I'm sure Ms Lewis is eager to hear the results of your tests.'

Maggie's brows furrowed. It was on the tip of her tongue to ask why Khalid was addressed in such a formal way. But she didn't want to prolong his presence with questions.

'Of course.' The older man approached the bed, his serious gaze caught her attention and she sat straighter, staring. It was impossible he'd found anything wrong with her. She was as healthy as a horse. Yet the tiny frown on the doctor's face sent anxiety pulsing through her.

'Is there something wrong?'

'No, no,' he assured her. 'Nothing wrong.' Yet the look he cast over his shoulder at Khalid looming nearby was clearly unsettled.

'I'll leave you alone,' Khalid said immediately.

'No!'

Two pairs of startled eyes fixed on her and Maggie chewed her lip. She'd never been a coward, had always faced life with all its problems and disappointments head-on. But if there was bad news, she felt a fervent, unreasoning wish that

Khalid be here too. She was in a strange country and he was a familiar face, she rationalised, blindly ignoring her own desire just moments ago to escape his dominant presence.

'Please stay,' she said, curving her lips into what she hoped was a smile.

Now the doctor looked really uncomfortable, his eyes sliding to the younger man, then away. Suddenly Maggie had a very bad feeling about this. She remembered her father's cancer being diagnosed and how, at the end, it had ravaged him beyond help.

'It's all right,' she assured the doctor, eager now to get this over and done with. Whatever the news, she'd rather know it now than wait on tenterhooks. 'Please tell me.'

The doctor nodded and cleared his throat. 'You're in excellent health, Ms Lewis. Apart from some bruising you're fine. However...' He paused and Maggie felt her heart sink.

'However, are you aware that you're pregnant?'

CHAPTER FIVE

'BUT I… It's not possible, surely.' Maggie's voice was breathless, her face tense with shock. 'Are you positive?'

Khalid knew Aziz too well to doubt. If he said she was pregnant, then Maggie Lewis was expecting a child.

His child.

The idea scraped a hollow in his chest.

Immediately he discarded the possibility that Maggie had gone from him to another man who'd got her pregnant. The idea was ludicrous. More than that, to his consternation he discovered it was untenable. Khalid couldn't imagine her in anyone else's bed. Just his own….

The realisation froze him into physical lockdown, his mind rejecting the gut-deep certainty. Warning lights flashed across his consciousness. Such possessiveness should be absurd. *Should* be. His chest heaved as he dragged in a slow, shuddering breath.

'I assure you, Ms Lewis, the test is positive. Congratulations.' The doctor's words and Maggie's response faded, drowned by the roar of blood in Khalid's ears.

Pregnant! This was one issue he'd never expected to confront. Not since his life had ripped apart eight years ago. Since then he'd plunged himself into a gruelling schedule of demanding projects rather than face the aching void inside him. When he found solace in a woman's company, he ensured the liaison was temporary. No entanglements, no complications.

A child…that was definitely a complication. A child meant family. Emotion. Love.

Khalid's jaw tightened, pain radiating from gritted teeth. He'd vowed never to go down that path again. He'd spent years avoiding anything that might develop into an emotionally intimate relationship. He'd wanted never to lay himself open to the risk of such anguish again.

That was the only safe way. The only way to survive.

The blur of emotion cleared and he saw Maggie, clinging to the chair with a white-knuckled grip. Her hazel eyes sparkled yet her face was too pale. She looked wan and shocked. She needed support. She needed *him*.

Not pausing to think, Khalid spun round, headed to the sink and poured a glass of water.

'Here. Drink.' It took a moment to catch her attention. Her fingers trembled as she took the glass. A surge of protectiveness washed over him.

Pregnant.

Regret stabbed him. Or was it guilt? Shahina had longed for a baby. She'd borne the news that she could never have children with a stoicism that had almost broken his heart. The one thing above all that his beloved wife had wanted and it had been denied her.

Yet, despite the poignant memories, it was satisfaction he felt deep in the pit of his belly. A kernel of pleased anticipation at the idea of his seed, his child, growing inside Maggie. His blood flowed effervescent and his heart pumped stronger and faster.

'But we took precautions,' Maggie said to the doctor.

Aziz shook his head. 'No precaution is foolproof, Ms Lewis. Nature has a way of succeeding in her purpose, no matter how hard we try to thwart her.'

Khalid considered the odds against that night leading to pregnancy. They'd made love only once and he'd been scrupulously careful to use a condom. And Maggie hadn't made love before. Her untutored caresses and tight, virginal body had been a potent aphrodisiac, tempting him to completion almost before he'd ensured her climax. Only the knowledge of her inexperience had prevented him turning to her again and again in the night.

There was no doubt this child was eager to come into the world. It must share its mother's indomitable spirit.

His gaze settled on Maggie, her slim form rigid. His emotions were jumbled and confusing. Yet above all there was a sense of rightness and of acceptance.

Khalid wanted this child.

'For now, I want you to rest,' Aziz said to Maggie. 'Your baby is safe and we'll continue to monitor its progress. We can discuss antenatal care later,' he added with a smile.

'Antenatal care?' Maggie's brow pleated in confusion and Khalid found himself wanting to step forward and soothe the frown from her face. Clearly the news had stunned her.

'Of course.' Aziz nodded. 'We'll need to discuss your diet among other things.'

'But I'm only here for a short time, to settle the horses in.'

Aziz looked from her to Khalid and Khalid knew he was trying to assess the situation between them. Khalid's presence here was unprecedented. It would be obvious to the meanest intelligence that this woman was special to him.

He stepped forward. 'Dr Aziz will see you tomorrow. No doubt by then you'll have questions for him. As for your stay in Shajehar, there must have been a misunderstanding. Your presence is required in the long term.'

'But my visa—'

'A new visa will be issued. Don't fret about it.'

Maggie watched the two men walk to the door, one comfortably plump and concerned, the other enigmatic and powerful. They conversed in their own language and she felt she'd missed something vital. Or perhaps shock made her imagine things.

Pregnant!

She sipped the water Khalid had brought and tried to marshal her thoughts. She couldn't believe it. The idea of children had been far into the nebulous future.

Panic tore through her, sucking her breath away. How would she manage? She knew nothing about babies. She'd been young when her sister was born. Nor did she have friends with young children. She'd lived too isolated a life; her father had seen to that. And she had precious little knowledge of 'normal' family life. She was alone, inexperienced and unprepared.

Money would be a problem too. She'd have to defer her plans to study. Her father had insisted she plough her earnings into saving the debt-ridden farm. With his death Maggie had given up the losing battle and begun saving instead for the future she'd always wanted.

Yet, despite the difficulties, Maggie knew absolutely that she wanted this baby. Already the thrill of excitement was overtaking stunned shock. She had no idea how she'd manage but there'd be time to sort that out later. Determination and joy welled inside her.

She'd have to scrimp and save and work hard and learn as she went. Nothing new there. And at the end of her pregnancy she'd have a precious child, family of her very own to love and care for.

A smile tickled her lips as she raised the glass once more. Crazy it might be, but she was excited.

'You're happy about the baby?' Khalid broke across her thoughts as he returned.

'It's…overwhelming,' she murmured as she met his gaze. Would their baby have eyes like his? Dark as jet and beautiful? Her pulse quickened. *Their baby*. It was incredible.

His stare was so steady, so intense that Maggie shivered,

wondering what he was thinking. His face was so still she could discern no expression.

'You're not…with someone, are you?' she blurted out as the horrifying idea surfaced. He wasn't married, but there were other sorts of commitments. 'Do you have a girlfriend? A fiancée?'

'No.' His voice was curt. 'I had a wife once. But there's no one now.'

He'd had a wife once…

Maggie stared up at his hard-edged face, transformed now into forbidding lines of aristocratic hauteur and disapproval.

Obviously his ex-wife wasn't a subject for discussion. Maggie wondered what the woman had done to deserve such disfavour.

'Why?' His expression was remote. 'Are you proposing?'

'Of course not!' Maggie heaved in a shocked breath. 'I just wondered… I don't want to cause trouble.' She paused, thinking. 'But then it won't matter, no one need know.'

Instantly Khalid's brows tilted together in a thunderous frown. 'You intend to dispose of our child? Is that what you're saying?'

Maggie edged back from the ferocious anger vibrating in his voice and put her glass down, not taking her eyes off him. His large hands fisted and his jaw looked honed of solid rock. She got to her feet and braced herself.

'No.' She shook her head till her hair swirled around her neck. 'How can you even suggest that?'

He regarded her intently, his flared nostrils and the rigid tendons in his neck proclaiming his tension.

'I don't know you,' he said eventually.

'Well, believe me, nothing would make me get rid of this baby.' She slipped her hand across her abdomen in a shielding gesture, overcome by wonder at this news and by the intense protectiveness she felt already for her child. She'd do everything she could to keep it safe.

His frown didn't ease and she felt like an insect scrutinised under a microscope, about to be dissected. She jutted her chin. He had no right to judge her.

'It's true. I want this baby.'

Our baby. But she couldn't say that, not when he looked at her with the eyes of a disapproving stranger. It was impossible to reconcile him with the generous, passionate man who'd taken her to paradise in his arms.

'Why do you want it?' He sounded like an interrogator, unconvinced and ready to believe the worst.

'I…' What could she say when she didn't know the answer herself? All she knew was that this child was part of her and she'd do anything to protect it.

'I don't believe in unwanted children,' she said at last. 'Every child should be wanted…and loved, by someone.' She'd spent most of her life knowing she wasn't loved, that her father only sheltered her out of grudging duty. She wouldn't wish that on anyone.

Her child would be loved absolutely and unconditionally. It would never know an instant's doubt about its special place in the world.

'I'll make sure this baby is loved and cared for.'

'That is not your responsibility.'

'Sorry?' His words brought her head swinging round to meet his gaze, ready to do battle.

'It is ours.'

Ours? Khalid's and hers? Her shoulders slumped in relief. For a moment there she'd thought he implied she wasn't fit to raise her own child.

'You want a role in bringing up this baby?'

'I will be involved in caring for *our* child.' Each word was clipped and definite. His posture, his look, proclaimed an arrogant certainty she secretly envied.

Maggie shook her head. Surely the difficulties of long-distance parenthood must outweigh the benefits.

'You'd deny me my rightful position as its father?'

He took a step forward and suddenly he was right there in front of her. Heat radiated from him and wrapped close around her. The scent of his skin invaded her space, overwhelming her attempts at rational thought. Instantly she was in bed, the smell of sandalwood and fresh male sweat tangy in her nostrils as he caressed her and drew her to shattering climax. Once more that secret, telltale heat ignited in the pit of her belly.

She closed her eyes, trying to master the surge of memory that shattered her thought processes. How could she think when he stood so close?

'It wouldn't work,' she murmured at last. 'It would be too difficult to manage.'

Warm fingers tilted her face up. Her eyes popped open and she met his gaze. It glowed with heat and something else, some burning emotion she couldn't define. For a moment absurd hope welled that perhaps he felt something for her. Something more than sympathy. She wanted that so badly it was a physical ache.

'Nothing is impossible, Maggie.'

The air sizzled as that spark, the connection she'd experienced only once before, arced between them. When he spoke like that, looked at her like that, she almost believed everything would turn out wonderfully.

Her heart accelerated to a hammering throb as she sank into the luxury of his heated gaze. Unthinking, she relaxed in his hold, slumping closer, drawn to his hard strength.

'We will find a way to make it work,' he murmured.

For all her prized ability to stand up for herself, this one man had the unerring ability to find weakness where none had existed. He made her feel she wasn't whole without him. She melted at his touch, even questioning the precepts she'd spent a lifetime learning: independence, pride and self-reliance.

Khalid was dangerous in ways she was only beginning to understand. She had to resist him and think rationally. Too much was at stake. Not merely her pride, but an innocent new life. Maggie jerked her chin from his hold, leaning back till his hand dropped away. Instantly she missed the warmth of his touch, craved its return.

'It's not that simple,' she argued.

His eyes narrowed to glittering slits and his challenging expression froze to implacable.

'Perhaps you'd like to explain why you're insistent I not take responsibility for my child.' He crossed his arms over his chest. The movement emphasised the spare power of his taut frame and gave him a threatening air.

Maggie looked away. It was far too easy to stare in helpless fascination at him. For all the belligerence of his stance, he was utterly mesmerising.

'Is it because I'm not from your country? Because I am a foreigner to you?'

Helplessly she shook her head. 'That's got nothing to do with it. It's just…' How did she explain that they were poles apart in wealth and status, in experience and expectations, without making it sound as if she were seeking reassurance? 'You're here and I'll be in Australia and—'

'Not necessarily.'

'Pardon?'

'We needn't be separated. For our child's sake, the sensible thing would be to stay together here.'

'Together?' she squawked. He couldn't mean what she thought. 'Together' didn't mean anything personal.

Still, it took far too long for her galloping heart rate to slow back to normal.

'That's not an option. I have to return home.'

'Perhaps I could persuade you.'

One sleek eyebrow rose questioningly and his lips quirked up at one corner in the merest hint of a smile. A pulse of heat throbbed deep inside her, impinging on her ability to think clearly. How did he do that?

Heaven help her if he ever deigned to smile properly. She'd dissolve into a puddle of molten desire at his feet. Maggie scrambled to compose herself.

'I'll be in Australia.'

'Do you really think that's best for our child? One parent in Australia and one in Shajehar?'

Anger unfurled in Maggie's belly at his calm question. She'd been rocked by today's news and was still grappling with the implications. Apparently Khalid had taken it in his stride. Unreasonably she resented that.

'You think you know what's best for the baby? Is that it? You're suddenly an expert with all the answers?'

She caught a glimpse of banked heat in his eyes. Was he so accustomed to deciding, always having his way? Did he expect her to accept his decision meekly?

'I don't pretend to be an expert, Maggie.' His voice was low and calm. 'I just know our child deserves the chance to be loved by both its parents.'

She felt as if he'd punched a hole through her indignation and her fear, right down to her secret, scared inner self. A desolate, black void of long-buried hurt yawned before her, threatening to suck her under. What did she know about parental love? She'd had so little of it.

For one panicked, sickening moment she wondered if the lack of love in her own childhood meant she was fated to be a poor parent herself. Was it possible? Could that sort of thing be inherited?

She gulped in an unsteady breath. Surely not. If anything the neglect she'd suffered meant she'd try harder to be a good mother.

'Maggie! What's the matter?'

Khalid watched her, his brow knitted with concern. Suddenly she was claustrophobic. This small room and his dominating presence were too much. She was used to being outdoors, on the move, not cooped up indoors.

'Can we leave here now?' she asked abruptly. 'We can talk this through later. I have to get back to the stables.' She stepped to one side, eager to escape the confines of the sick-bay and Khalid's scrutiny. Surely they could put off this conversation till she was more in control of her emotions.

But he didn't budge. The set of his jaw told her he wasn't going anywhere. His proximity was daunting. Her breath shortened, but she refused to back down.

'Look.' She angled her face up to meet his impenetrable stare, steeling herself not to flinch. 'We have lots to discuss, I know. Lots to work out. I'm not trying to avoid you. But wouldn't it make more sense to talk this through later? Somewhere private where we're not likely to be interrupted?' That would give her time to adjust to the news and marshal her thoughts.

'If I'm not back at work soon, my boss will be furious. I've already been gone for ages. It's a wonder he hasn't stormed in here demanding I get back to the stables. What we have to discuss is too important for interruption.'

Her heart thudded as Khalid watched her silently. Eventually he inclined his head.

'You're right. This isn't the most appropriate place for our conversation. As for being interrupted, you need have no fear. No one will intrude on us.'

'You don't know the stable manager. He's—'

'No one you need worry about.'

At her astonished stare Khalid's lips curved up into that delicious quirk, then slowly spread to a full-blown smile that made the pulse thunder in her ears and her nerves jangle in awareness.

He was utterly, indescribably magnetic. He was far more vibrant, more potently attractive than any man had a right to be. Her breath snared and she swayed, feeling the full impact of that attraction.

A firm hand grasped her by the elbow and turned her towards the door. The heat of his touch sizzled like summer lightning across her skin.

'I see you haven't caught up with the latest news, Maggie. You don't know who I am, do you?'

'Your name's Khalid,' she murmured, unsettled by the glint in his eyes. 'You were the sheikh's envoy.'

He nodded. 'I was. Now my position has changed. Four weeks ago I became Sheikh of Shajehar. You're an honoured guest in *my* palace. *My* country.'

Maggie sat quietly in the ornate garden pavilion as Khalid thanked the servant who'd brought refreshments. Then he conversed briefly with a man in an expensive suit who obviously had important news.

She was grateful for the respite, was still reeling from the shock of Khalid's identity. Even now she couldn't quite believe it!

Yet watching him she wondered that she hadn't guessed the truth. He had the face of a storybook prince: strong, commanding and aristocratic. More than that, his air of authority, of uncompromising power, was unmistakable.

Hadn't she seen him with her own eyes, about to sit on the gilded throne at the centre of the ringside stand? Hadn't she heard the doctor refer to him as 'sire'?

Khalid, the man who'd made tender, tempestuous love to her weeks ago, the man who'd cared for her when she was distraught, the man who'd leapt into the ring today and taken control of Diva…was the royal Sheikh of Shajehar.

'My apologies, Maggie. My chancellor had a few urgent matters that required attention.'

'That's OK.' She nodded, though she felt completely out of her depth. She didn't have a clue what a chancellor did, much less a monarch. The opulent luxury of the pavilion with its silk-covered divans, exquisite murals and breathtaking views to the indigo mountains only reinforced the fact that she didn't belong here.

She'd never seen the previous Sheikh on his visits to Australia, but his wealth and power were legend. It was rumoured he'd had a silver Rolls-Royce. Not silver-coloured but made of silver. That he bought entire luxury resorts so he could holiday in private. More than that, here in Shajehar his word was law. He'd been an absolute ruler.

As Khalid was now.

That was the sort of man who'd fathered her child. A man of wealth and power beyond her imaginings. A man who could buy anything he wanted.

Suddenly fear jolted through her. If he wanted the baby badly enough, could he take it from her?

'I won't give up my baby.' The words were out before she'd even had time to consider them.

Khalid paused in the act of passing her a glass of tea and raised his brows. 'No one is asking you to, Maggie.'

Relief swamped her. She'd grown up without her mother and she wouldn't inflict that on her baby. That permanent sense of loss, the sadness for missed intimacies and love and laughter. The lingering self-doubt, that maybe it was something she'd done that had driven her mum away. Maggie had missed so much, not having a mother to share her hopes and fears and guide her as she grew from girl to woman.

'Good.' She refused to apologise. 'I just thought it better you knew up front.'

He nodded. 'And you should know that I will not walk away from our child, either. Here.' He pressed the glass into her hand. 'Drink up. It'll do you good.'

Maggie inhaled the familiar aroma of sweet tea, Shajehani style, and remembered Khalid telling her once before that it was good for shock. She hoped he was right.

'I can recommend the pastries too.'

She looked at the perfectly presented delicacies. Could the tray really be solid gold?

'Not at the moment, thank you.' Instead she sipped her tea

gratefully. But the sensation of his eyes on her made her look up. He watched her so intently.

'You have no cause to fear me, Maggie. I'm a civilised man.'

'A civilised man who rules his own country and can buy the best lawyers in the world.' She bit her lip, willing herself to shut up before she dug herself any deeper.

'That's not how I work!' There was a flash of fury in his eyes before he looked away towards the distant view. Instantly regret filled her, but she had to be sure.

'I didn't ask to be sheikh, didn't expect it. But my half-brother died without a son so I shoulder the role.'

'I'm sorry about your brother.'

He inclined his head and she paused, searching for words.

'You don't sound as if you enjoy your new position.' Which was probably tactless, and definitely not royal protocol. But their relationship certainly wasn't normal. And she needed to understand him.

'I will never shirk my duty,' he said in a low voice. 'There is much to do here. In the past my family were true leaders and visionaries, protecting their people. But—' his expression tightened '—since the discovery of oil, our rulers devoted themselves to squandering the country's wealth. It's my task to make up for years of neglect. To rectify the damage. It will be my lifetime's work.'

Now she understood. Khalid was a man of honour, driven by duty. 'You see our baby as your responsibility. Your duty.' She slipped a hand over her abdomen.

'Together we are responsible for that new life growing inside you.' At his words she felt heat unfurl within her, a tingle of excitement and awe. Her lips curved up in a faint smile. She still found the news wondrous.

'So together we must make the best arrangements for our child's future.'

She looked up, wary at his portentous tone. His heavy-lidded eyes gleamed with a sultry, unfamiliar heat.

'There's an obvious solution,' he continued.

'There is?' Her heart pounded and her nerves stretched thin as something like fear awoke in her breast.

'Of course.' His lips curled up at the corners in a satisfied smile. 'We will marry as soon as possible.'

CHAPTER SIX

KHALID was ready for Maggie's reaction: sheer, stunned silence. He knew that in her world people usually married for love. That children were often born out of wedlock.

Hadn't he married for love himself? Then vowed never to marry again, after losing Shahina tore his soul in two?

Nevertheless, the dawning horror in Maggie's eyes irked him. She hadn't found him so repulsive when she'd offered herself to him just weeks ago. And he knew any number of women who'd do almost anything to elicit his proposal. Some had already tried.

'You're... Are you serious?' Her voice was husky.

Khalid clamped down on rising anger. 'It is the most appropriate way forward.'

'The most appropriate.' Her lush mouth twisted. What did she expect? That he'd turn his back on her and the child? That he wouldn't care about them? She could hardly expect a declaration of undying love. Besides, that was something he could never give any woman.

'Maggie, think about it. Our child will be born into a family. It will have two parents that love it. He or she will grow up in a stable environment, not hauled across continents and cultures, divided between distant parents.' He watched the green flecks darken her eyes.

'And you will have wealth, security, status.' All the things so many women desired.

'What if I'm not interested in money or status?'

Khalid pursed his lips against a smug grin. If she'd been the sort to chase him for his wealth this situation would have been different. But he knew Maggie Lewis was no gold-digger. Even the investigator who'd located her had said she was poor but hardworking, honest and reliable.

'Think of what this will mean for our baby. Isn't that most important? You said your father brought you up alone and it wasn't the happiest of situations. How much better for our child with both of us to care for him or her?'

He watched her chew her lip and felt a spurt of triumph. And a surge of sensual awareness. 'We have that in common, remember? My father wasn't a good parent, either. But we two together could provide the sort of home neither of us had ourselves.'

'But there's no guarantee it will work. What if we marry then separate? That can shatter a child.'

Khalid took her hand, smoothing his thumb over her skin. Her bones were fine, yet she was strong. He took it as a victory that she didn't pull back.

'You have my word, Maggie, that I would never drive you away or ask you to leave. You have my bond that I intend to work at building a warm, loving home for our child. And since we're not marrying for love, then our relationship won't be cluttered with emotion. We won't have the power to hurt each other as lovers can.'

The more he thought about it, the more perfect this arrangement sounded. Yet he read doubt in her eyes.

'But what if you fall in love with someone else?' She shook her head. 'No, marriage is a recipe for disaster.'

Strange, he thought, that she didn't consider the possibility she might fall for someone. Not that he had concerns in that regard. He knew how to keep a woman satisfied and happy. Maggie wouldn't be looking at other men while she had him.

'I am not the sort to lose my heart. You can be absolutely sure of that,' he murmured, determination firming his lips. His heart was well guarded now. He had no intention of ever opening it again.

Yet, still, she wasn't satisfied. 'Why do you want to marry? Is it so you have a legitimate heir?'

'You believe it's wrong to give our child the security of two parents and the protection of my name?' Khalid straightened in anger. Couldn't she see this was best? There was nothing shameful in his proposal.

'No, of course not,' she said slowly.

'Good. I have no intention of allowing our child to be born illegitimate.'

Khalid knew too well the unwanted implications of that. If his Uncle Hussein had been legitimate, instead of the fruit of a brief liaison between Khalid's grandfather and a dancer, Hussein would have been Sheikh. Honest, serious, hardworking, he would have been an excellent ruler. Instead the crown had passed to his younger, feckless, legitimate brother, Khalid's father, a shallow man, wrapped up in his own importance and with an obsession for personal gratification. As a direct result Shajehar had suffered all these years.

'So you want an heir.' Her voice was disapproving.

He shrugged. 'If I have no child the sheikhdom will pass to someone else in my family. But there *is* a child. Or there will be.' He darted a glance at her flat belly and a stab of wonderment shafted through him at the idea of her swelling as his child grew inside her.

A visceral, possessive sense of ownership filled him. This was *his* baby. And Maggie Lewis, though she didn't know it yet, was *his* woman. Already the sexual pull between them was too strong to deny. A single look was all it took to ignite roaring need inside him.

'Would you deny our baby its birthright? The chance to know its father's culture? Would you stop it from taking its rightful place here?'

'You're assuming it will be a boy.'

'No, you're the one making the assumptions.' He released her hand and surged to his feet, striding away, then spinning round to face her. 'I will love our baby if it is a boy or a girl. If it has pale skin and gold hair like yours or olive skin like mine. What matters is that it is our baby and we do the best for it.'

He looked at her as she sat, tea clasped in one tense hand. Despite her obdurate front this woman needed gentle handling. Pain, as well as strength, coloured her view of the world. Her eyes still revealed the shock of Aziz's news.

Silently he cursed his tendency to instant action. When he saw his way ahead, he never delayed. Perhaps this time he should have tempered his response and given her a chance to absorb the implications of her pregnancy.

Her pregnancy. His child.

He stepped close and took the glass from her. 'Come, Maggie. We will talk of this later. It's time you rested.'

Maggie was hot and dirty and weary. Yesterday's revelations still stunned her. She could barely believe she was going to be a mother! Yet her excitement was tempered by a morass of confused emotions.

Nor had her mood improved when she'd arrived at the stables this morning to discover she'd been ordered onto light duties. A day of menial tasks and curious stares had done nothing to rebuild her equanimity. Her every move was watched, assessed, speculated over.

'Come on, Tally.' She led the mare through the yard to the horses' swimming pool. Tally's ears flicked forward and her nostrils widened as she scented water.

'Maggie!'

She stopped mid-stride, held fast by that voice. Khalid's

tone was commanding. Her heart pump faster, knowing he was here, watching her. She felt his stare, like a hot knife blade between her shoulders.

Slowly she turned. He stood framed in the shadows of the arched gateway. The late-afternoon sun gilded his long, pale robe. It highlighted his superb breadth of shoulder, the tensile strength of his tall frame, the breath-stealing male beauty of his stern face.

The hiss of her indrawn breath was loud in her ears as she stared in helpless fascination and felt her instant response. It was as she'd feared. A flare of excitement, of anticipation, sparked deep within her at the sight of him. It didn't matter that he was angry. His scowl only emphasised his strong features and his air of authority.

She'd never liked domineering men. Had vowed never to fall into the trap of caring for a man like her father. But, despite the potent masculine power that fair sizzled off Khalid, Maggie couldn't douse her thrill of pleasure. The air between them sparked with enough energy to light his vast palace. She couldn't drag her eyes away.

'Hello, Khalid.' She hated her breathless voice. She'd been expecting another summons, not the man himself.

He paced across the sun-warmed pavement and something sank inside her as his stride ate up the distance. Her only hope had been that she wouldn't be affected by his presence as before. That hope shattered as she stood, held in thrall. Now she knew: her response was dangerously real.

'I asked you to come and see me.' His narrowed gaze trawled over her and heat blossomed under her skin in its wake. She tried to look nonchalant.

'Did you? That's odd. The message I received didn't sound like an invitation. It was more like a royal decree.'

It took every ounce of strength to meet his glinting eyes. Now she was paying for her refusal twenty minutes ago to obey his summons instantly.

After a sleepless night she was still confused and anxious, unsure what to do for the best. All day she'd expected to see him, had been taut with nerves, preparing to face him again. Yet he'd kept his distance. No doubt he had other, more important things on his mind than her pregnancy!

'And yet you chose not to come.' His voice was cool, his expression composed, but she felt anger in him as he stopped, far too close for her peace of mind.

Tally must have sensed her agitation for the horse started forward towards the ramp that led down into the pool and Maggie had to work at holding her steady.

'I'm not a subject to come at your bidding.'

His sudden stillness told her that barb had hit home.

'But you *are* my employee,' he said eventually, his voice low. 'Or doesn't that matter?'

Maggie blinked, reeling that he'd choose to use her position here to bring her to heel. What was between them was personal and private.

'My apologies, *boss*.' She almost choked on the word. 'I hadn't realised you wanted to discuss my work.'

He raised a hand and massaged the back of his neck, as if to soothe away a knot of tension. The blood thundering in her ears pounded out the passing seconds of silence.

'I'm sorry, Maggie. That was uncalled for,' he said at last. 'I apologise.'

He looked so uncomfortable that she felt a swell of sympathy for him. Was he as unsettled by this situation as she? No doubt he was used to making demands that those around him were eager to meet. Especially women. She'd guess they'd be only too happy to deal with his requests, no matter how *demanding*. The idea created a niggle of discomfort so intense it dismayed her.

'Accepted,' she said quickly. 'I was going to come to you as soon as I'd finished here.' She avoided his eyes. 'I take my work very seriously.'

'You think the matter between us isn't serious?' His tone told her he wasn't used to people refusing to comply with his wishes. That straightened her backbone.

'I assumed you didn't need to see me urgently, since you waited all day.'

'Ah.' He paused for so long she wondered if he had no reply. 'Again I must beg your pardon, Maggie. I've been with representatives of two neighbouring countries while we negotiate multilateral agreements on trade and regional infrastructure.' His voice dropped to a deep pitch that unravelled some of the tightness in her shoulders. 'I wanted to see you earlier but it was impossible. The meetings were organised months ago.'

Which made Maggie feel smaller and less significant than ever. Of course he'd had a good reason not to see her. It was stupid to be piqued at his lack of attention.

'Do you mind if I take Tally in?' she asked abruptly, nodding to the deep channel of water. 'She loves her swim.'

'And when you've done this, you'll finish for the day.' It was a statement, not a question. Maggie had the suspicion that even if she hadn't finished, Khalid would ensure she stopped. 'Please, go ahead. I'll walk with you.'

She turned and led the mare into the water. Maggie walked beside the pool as Tally hurried down the ramp and into the channel sunk below ground level. Soon the horse was swimming in the deep water, kicking out strongly.

'Marriage is the best option. You know that, Maggie.'

No preliminaries, no hesitancy. Was Khalid always so supremely sure of himself?

Didn't he see how preposterous his suggestion was? As if it were totally logical for her, a girl who worked in the stables, to marry a man who ruled his own country.

'Not from my perspective,' she murmured. She kept her head averted, watching the mare.

'My manager hasn't spoken to you yet about my plans for the stables, has he?'

She jerked her head around. He walked beside her, closer than she'd realised. His eyes were grave.

'What plans?' Anxiety shivered down her backbone.

'Your job at Tallawanta will end in the near future.'

Her mouth dried. 'What do you mean?'

'I'm disposing of the stud. While there's so much to be achieved here in Shajehar I don't have the stomach for such luxuries, even successful ones. Which means...' he paused, surveying her carefully '...that your job in Australia will no longer exist. The stud's new owners may need you or they may decide to bring in their own staff.'

Foreboding ratcheted up Maggie's pulse and she faltered. Cold sweat prickled her nape at the thought of her job disappearing.

Her arm jerked as Tally swam ahead and Maggie tried to concentrate on the mare. But her thoughts circled around Khalid's news. She needed her job to support her baby. Good positions were scarce and she had no other qualifications.

Surely he wasn't doing this to force her hand?

'I'd decided to sell it, and several of Faruq's other indulgences, well before we met.'

Had he read her mind and the doubt hovering there?

'But I need a steady job for the baby, and to save so I can train one day as a vet.' Even as she said it she realised how unlikely that dream was. Looking after her child had to be her priority now.

'There's a fine university here in Shajehar. Veterinary study is one of its specialties.'

Sure, as if she could enrol. She couldn't even speak the language. Maggie pursed her lips in a derisory grimace.

'So I should stay here because it would be easier than finding a new job?' She couldn't keep the bitterness from her tone. She felt as if he'd pulled the whole fabric of her world askew. She was adrift on a sea of uncertainty.

Maggie urged the mare on, wishing she could run ahead,

outpace Khalid and absorb this news alone. But solitude was a luxury she didn't have anymore. Whether she wanted it or not, Khalid was determined to be involved in her future.

Correction, their child's future. The two were inextricably linked. Claustrophobia encompassed her, binding round her till she could barely breathe.

Tally surged up the ramp and out of the deep swimming channel. Even the comical sight of the mare shaking herself like a dog didn't make Maggie smile. She felt overwhelmed.

'Maggie?' Khalid stepped in front of her, straight into her line of vision. 'You will have a new job whether you like it or not. Being a mother will be very demanding.'

She shook her head in amazement. 'And you think it will be easier for me if I emigrate, tie myself to a man I barely know and marry into a royal family?'

'You would not be alone. You would want for nothing.' His tone was patient, warm and reassuring.

Yet she'd run the risk of losing what little she had achieved for herself. Her independence, her plans for the future.

Though perhaps it was inevitable. Her future wasn't her own anymore. A shiver of panicked excitement shot through her as this new reality struck her again. *Pregnant*. Maggie breathed deep and calmed herself.

'I don't fit your world.' She waved a dismissive hand over herself. Her boots were dusty, her trousers splashed and liberally sprinkled with horse hair. 'I don't belong in a palace. I'm ordinary. I work for my living.'

His eyes held hers and a pulse of something unexpected beat between them. Connection.

'As do I, Maggie.'

Instantly she regretted her words. Already she'd learned how seriously Khalid took his responsibilities.

'I'm sorry, Khalid. I know you do. But our circumstances are different.' She tethered the mare, reaching for a plastic scraper and beginning to dry Tally's wet coat. It gave her the perfect excuse not to look at him. She focused on the slide of the plastic over Tally's body, sluicing the water away. If only it were as easy to remove one large, stubborn male from her vicinity.

'Surely you need to marry someone who will fit in.'

'You will fit in, Maggie.' He took a step towards her. The world narrowed to *him*. His glowing eyes, his rangy power, his presence. Her heart pounded against her ribs.

'I'll be right here with you.' His voice dropped to a soft rumble that made her insides squirm with pleasure.

She shook her head, denying the shiver of tentative delight. He didn't understand at all! How could she marry a man who saw their wedding as 'the most appropriate way forward'? Who didn't love her and never would? She'd be mad to tie herself to such an arrangement.

'I mean, you must be expected to marry someone—' she swallowed her pride '—beautiful and elegant, groomed for the position. Someone from an important family.'

As he watched she squared her shoulders and lifted her chin. It was body language he recognised, a stance he'd used himself as a child when ordered to some irksome duty.

She didn't hide behind the usual female prevarication. She was so transparent he felt a moment's qualm for her vulnerability. But that couldn't sway him. He intended to have her as his bride, by persuasion if possible.

'The sheikhs of Shajehar have a reputation for marrying to please themselves.'

He conveniently omitted to mention the tentative negotiations Faruq had instigated just months ago to cement a dynastic match between Khalid and a princess from a neighbouring kingdom. Khalid had been opposed to the idea from the start. He'd never wanted to marry again.

Until now.

This was necessary. Marriage was his duty to his unborn child. Fate had given him this opportunity for a child and he could no more turn his back on it than stop breathing. He knew exactly how precious life was and he intended to be an integral part of his child's world.

That meant having Maggie too. He felt surprisingly reconciled to the idea.

'No one will believe you want me.' Her voice was cool, but her mouth had a vulnerable slant.

Maggie stepped aside, turning to work on the horse. Her movements were smooth and rhythmic, almost but not quite concealing the tension that gripped her.

The dying sun lit her hair to old gold. It outlined her sleek curves and lissom body. Heat shot through him at the memory of those endless legs encompassing him the night he took her virginity. Of her exquisite body coming to life for the first time at his touch. Maggie was so wonderfully responsive, so endlessly enticing.

He might not be marrying for love this time, but there was no doubt he wanted this marriage. He *wanted* Maggie. All these weeks, through the turmoil of taking up his role as Sheikh, he'd missed her. More than he should have.

Missed the woman he'd known for just one night!

Marriage was his duty—obvious and unavoidable. But not entirely simple. He thought of her passion, her vitality, how she'd roused him and satisfied him, then made him hunger for her again with a desperate intensity that was entirely new.

This marriage would be about pleasure too. As Maggie would soon discover.

He stepped close and felt her heat through the fine linen of his clothes. Instantly an answering fire scorched his flesh, drawing it taut with sexual anticipation.

'No one will question my choice, Maggie. They will know as soon as they see you that I want you.'

She swung round to face him, her hazel-gold eyes wide with astonishment. And something more. A flicker of pain.

'Don't. They'd take one look and know that for a lie.'

Had she never looked in the mirror? Never recognised the heady eroticism of her own body? The bone-deep beauty, the elegance and allure? Had she truly no idea how gut-wrenchingly sexy she was in slim-fitting trousers, her face pure of artificial embellishment?

Heat pooled low in his body, his groin tightening, his arousal burgeoning heavily. It would be the work of a moment to reach out and haul her against him. Show her exactly how much he wanted her.

But that shadow of anguish in her expression stopped him. This was difficult enough for her. Pregnant, in a foreign country, still grappling with the idea of marriage. She looked ready to take flight. He had to proceed slowly.

'Clothes can be changed. They are nothing.' Instantly a vision filled his mind of her standing there, absolutely naked, for his personal delectation.

Every muscle froze at the potent image.

He drew in a sharp breath and continued before his good intentions deserted him and he resorted to a more earthy form of persuasion.

'I will treat you with respect. I will treat you as my wife. There will be no doubt in anyone's mind.'

She shook her head. 'You mean, the respect the mother of your child deserves.' Her words had a wasp-sharp sting.

'That too,' he murmured. He read Maggie's set face and changed tack. 'I can promise you respect and loyalty. Is that such a bad bargain?' Ruthlessly he tightened the net. 'What do you have to go home to? Is there so much waiting for you there you can't give it up for a new life?'

He didn't need to say more. The truth lay stark and unrelenting between them. No one waited for her. Her own country held nothing except unemployment, loneliness and the struggle of single parenthood.

'But we have nothing in common,' she said at last, her mouth a flat line, her eyes averted.

Khalid repressed a smile. He'd won, though she might not admit it yet. Spears of hot anticipation lanced him.

He steered away from mentioning their explosive sexual compatibility. Instinct told him she found that unsettling. Time enough to deal with that when they were wed. He looked forward to that day. To alleviating the heady arousal he experienced whenever he was with her.

'We will find that with time,' he assured her. 'For now we have our child and our honesty. That's a better beginning than many.'

'Here you go, sweetie.' Maggie gave the little boy a boost up into the saddle of the sturdy pony.

It didn't matter that he didn't speak English nor she Arabic. His grin told her all she needed to know. Quickly she checked his feet were in the stirrups and that he held his reins properly. She motioned for him to straighten his back and shoulders, smiling and nodding approval as he did.

When she reached for the leading-rein a torrent of outraged protest issued from his lips.

'Don't pay any attention, Maggie.' Khalid's voice came from just beside her. 'Hamed knows he's not ready to ride alone yet.'

Maggie flashed her rider a look that indicated she wouldn't brook any nonsense, then dropped the lead-rein, leaving the pony standing tethered. There was instant silence as Hamed realised he wasn't going anywhere just yet.

'He'll be OK.' She turned to Khalid. 'It's just his pride talking. I'll give him a moment.'

Khalid's smile was warm and Maggie felt the tension of the past forty-eight hours slip away. This afternoon spent with Khalid and his cousin's brood of children had been more fun than she'd expected. Not once had he mentioned marriage, though his proposal stood between them, silent and unavoidable. As always, being with children had lightened her mood.

She'd revelled in their excitement at visiting the ponies Khalid kept for them.

'You know about young boys.' Was that approval she heard?

She shrugged. 'Back home I help out with a programme for disabled riders. We meet every second Saturday and most of the riders are children. I've picked up a thing or two.'

'You enjoy being with children?'

'Of course. What's not to like?' Kids took you as they found you. They were open and honest about their feelings.

'Have you always wanted children?'

'I...suppose so.' His eyes held her so she couldn't look away. 'It wasn't something I'd planned just yet.' She grimaced. This pregnancy was anything but planned. 'But I'd always assumed I'd have children. One day, when I met...'

'The right man.'

Silently she nodded, rocked again by the vast difference between reality and her secret hopes of everlasting love. It was time to forget her dream of finding a man who'd love her for herself. She had to think now of her baby, not pie-in-the-sky romantic dreams.

'How about you? Did you want children?'

His face was still, suddenly sombre. 'It wasn't a lifetime ambition, but yes, I've wanted children.'

Maggie didn't understand the shadow of pain in his eyes. Khalid wasn't a simple man to understand.

She turned back to Hamed with an encouraging smile. Soon she was leading him round the stable yard, reminding him to sit still while he chattered nineteen to the dozen.

But as they walked it was Khalid who held her attention. Khalid standing with little Ayisha in his arms, showing her how to feed a carrot to one of the horses. There was a squeal of delight as the mare snuffled up the treat and Ayisha giggled. Alone of all the children, Ayisha had been timid with the ponies.

Maggie watched Khalid cradle the child against his strong

frame and felt something give way inside her. The big man and the tiny girl were so perfect together.

She heard his murmured encouragement, saw his swift movement to prevent Ayisha lunging recklessly at the horse's head. He was patient, gentle, caring. Khalid would be a doting parent, but no pushover. Their child would have boundaries but plenty of love too. If she married him.

That was what she wanted for their child. Not the constrained existence she'd led, always anticipating her father's disapproval, his temper. Khalid was nothing like her father. He'd encourage, not destroy youthful aspirations. For all his power and wealth, Khalid would make the sort of father she wanted for their baby.

Her breath expelled in a sigh. Could she commit to a loveless marriage when she'd craved love all her life?

She couldn't allow it to matter. She'd do whatever it took to give her baby the best.

Khalid would never love her, never regard her as anything other than the mother of his child. His 'proposal' had left it baldly obvious his emotions would never be engaged. This was about the baby. About legitimacy, honour and duty.

He kept his distance, never touched her now. Any marriage would be in name only. She'd have to find a way to stop the surge of physical longing she felt for him. She bit her lip. Maybe it was because she'd been a virgin till so recently. Perhaps this…desire that haunted even her dreams would cease with time.

'You look very serious.'

Maggie found Khalid blocking her path, Ayisha still in his arms. The sight made her think about him holding their child. Of the love and support he'd give it in abundance.

She drew to a halt and Hamed's pony nuzzled her side.

'I was thinking.'

Was that a flash of something in his dark eyes or a trick of the light?

'Thinking about us,' he murmured. 'About the baby.'

He was so sure of himself she wanted to deny it. But what was the point? Of course she'd been thinking about them. It was all she thought about, wondering what to do for the best. Scared to trust herself to a stranger, but forced to acknowledge the benefits for their baby.

'You've decided.' His stare imprisoned her. 'Tell me.'

Maggie's heart rose in her throat. She'd finally made her decision.

'Yes, Khalid. I'll marry you.'

CHAPTER SEVEN

BARELY two weeks later Maggie stood in front of the full-length mirror in her luxurious new suite of rooms. Amazement filled her at the stranger she saw there. It was incredible what a fortune in clothes and jewellery and the attentions of a small army of women could achieve.

There wasn't so much as a whiff of the stables clinging to this royal bride.

Uncertain, she walked closer, aware with every step of the unfamiliar weight and the stiff formality of the cloth-of-gold fabric embroidered with pearls. Someone with an eye for her colouring had insisted on emeralds for her jewellery. They made her eyes sparkle.

Or was that trepidation? The butterflies in her stomach were the size of giant condors and her second thoughts took up most of her time.

And yet… She stared at the woman in the mirror and wondered. Could she make this work? If she could look the part maybe, one day, she could grow into the role of sheikh's wife. And she did look—

'Magnificent!'

She spun round in a flurry of long skirts, her pulse jumping.

'Khalid! What are you doing here?'

He'd been leaning against the doorjamb. Now he straightened and paced towards her. He looked every inch the royal sheikh. More, he looked like her fantasy prince come to life: lithe, gorgeous and dangerously intense. His splendid robes emphasised the lean elegance of his masculine frame.

The look in his eyes made her blood sizzle.

'I'm admiring my bride.' He halted in front of her. His intent scrutiny made her heart pump harder.

'But are you supposed to be here?'

'Where else would I be on our wedding day?'

His gaze dropped, travelling slowly over her flushed cheeks, lingering on her mouth. She snatched a breath. Her lips throbbed and parted and his eyes narrowed. Heat flared across her skin at the intensity of that look.

He surveyed every inch of her from the ornate gossamer-thin silk veil covering her hair, down to the full-length gown. A little earlier, being dressed in all her finery, Maggie had felt like an impostor. The luxurious fabrics and the wealth of jewels weren't for the likes of her. Yet as his gaze heated her skin to a white-hot sizzle she let herself wonder, just for a moment, what he really thought of his bride. His eyes lingered on the emeralds, heavy at her ears and breast.

Slowly he smiled. If she hadn't known better, she'd have said it was a proprietorial smile. Like a man coveting a secret treasure. Yet that was impossible.

She frowned, trying to concentrate on something other than the desperate yearning she felt for this man. He wanted her only as the necessary means to obtain his child. Lust for her husband was not an option.

'Isn't it bad luck for the groom to see his bride before the wedding?'

'Luck?' he scoffed. 'We make that for ourselves. Besides, you are alone on a day when a woman looks to her family and friends for support.'

He stepped close and took her hand, his warmth enfolding her. 'You have no family and you didn't invite any friends to the wedding. So I am here to take their place. I didn't want you to be alone, Maggie.'

The timbre of his voice was low and rich and warm, sending a frisson of emotion through her.

She'd expected him to be kind, and she knew him to be generous, but she hadn't thought he really cared.

'Thank you, Khalid.' The words seemed woefully insufficient.

He squeezed her fingers and the churning in her stomach eased just a fraction.

'You're right. It's better not to be alone.' She'd spent too long today fretting over old hurts, wondering where her mother and sister were. Her attempts to trace them hadn't got far and she had no idea where they were. The stab of disappointment had been sharp. She'd always dreamed of having her mother at her wedding day. Of her sister, Cassie, standing up as her bridesmaid.

This morning, even surrounded by chattering ladies-in-waiting primping and fussing over her outfit, she'd felt horribly alone.

She forced a smile to her lips and met Khalid's eyes.

'I'm gaining a new family,' she said, her hand smoothing low over the lush fabric covering her abdomen. 'It's a new beginning.'

Khalid saw the determination in her steady gaze, the strength of purpose, as well as the shadows of pain. He slid her arm through his, drawing her close.

'You honour me, Maggie. I will make sure you never regret it.'

How different was this wedding day, this bride, compared to his first marriage.

Then there'd been festivities and family celebrations for months before. He'd felt the buzz of excitement, anticipation and heady expectancy. A sense of adventure as he and the woman he adored embarked on their life together.

This time there were no hearts involved. He and Maggie were simply making a sensible, considered commitment for the sake of their child.

That didn't stop him wanting to wipe her hurt away.

He curled a finger under her chin and lifted her face. Her eyes glowed brighter than the gems she wore and he felt a shaft of heat pierce him. He was looking forward to their wedding night. He'd ached for her for weeks.

'Trust me. Just relax and don't worry about anything.'

'So, wife, what do you think of our Shajehani wedding celebrations?'

Maggie sat straighter in her seat as Khalid's warm breath feathered her cheek, detonating a whole series of explosive sensations through her body. The way he said 'wife' in that low tone made her pulse throb and her nipples peak with secret pleasure. His voice was a rumble of sound that reminded her of the night they'd become lovers. His scent teased her, evocative and arousing.

'It's spectacular,' she said. 'Just stunning. I hadn't expected anything like this.'

Ever since she'd agreed to the wedding, Khalid had kept his distance. They'd met only in the presence of others. There'd been no private words. No chance to retract her promise. Until today when he'd prowled into her room with the casual insouciance of…she stifled shocked laughter…of a sheikh visiting his harem! But today had been about supporting her, that was all. Despite that single searing look, Khalid had been a model of decorum ever since. He'd merely been concerned for her welfare.

To her dismay she found herself regretting that this marriage was to be a formality. With Khalid so close, that skittering sensual excitement quickened her blood again. She wanted him, in every way a woman wanted a man. But she'd tied herself into a bloodless union!

'I'm glad you approve,' he murmured.

Avoiding the temptation to turn and meet his eyes, she gazed out over the throng. She'd never seen so many people in one place. The vast open-sided tent was crammed with people and the noise was a constant din. Beyond the main tent people spread as far as she could see, seated on rugs, lit by ornate braziers. The smell of roast meat and spices filled the air. The sound of music and laughter. A hubbub of conversation and goodwill.

'They don't seem to mind your choice of bride,' she said tentatively. 'Everyone has been friendly.' It had been a relief to find some familiar faces, like Khalid's uncle Hussein and his wife, Zeinab, who had taken Maggie under her wing and begun teaching her Shajehani customs.

'Of course they approve. They wouldn't question my choice.' For all his talk of progress and his desire to modernise the country, the arrogance in Khalid's tone was that of an autocrat, superbly sure of himself.

A ripple of unease feathered down her spine. How well did she know the man she'd married?

'They can see you are a woman worthy of their sheikh. You are beautiful tonight, Maggie.' His voice dropped to a deep whisper, so low it vibrated right through her.

Despite her best intentions she gave in to the need that clawed at her, to take her fill of the sight of him, to bask in his nearness. Slowly she turned. His glittering eyes, dark as midnight, met hers and her heart turned over with a thud she could almost hear.

'You don't need to say that, Khalid. I don't need to be humoured.'

'Humoured?' His sleek eyebrows arrowed down. 'You must learn to trust me, Maggie. I do not lie.'

But he exaggerated. She appreciated his kindness. He was trying to reassure her and boost her self-confidence.

He leaned close. 'Your eyes are like stars. Your mouth is sweet invitation. Your throat is as delicate as—'

'Khalid! Please!' she hissed. She tried to prevent the delight that rippled through her at his words and, more, at his heavy-lidded look. 'Don't!'

'Don't what?' His mouth twisted in a tight hard curve that she didn't understand. He looked annoyed.

'Please, don't say things like that.' She darted a glance over her shoulder, but for once everyone seemed absorbed in their meal, their conversation, and not in their prince and his bride. She could only be thankful as heat flushed her cheeks, then ebbed away.

'As you wish.' He paused, only speaking again when she turned round to face him. 'So, what shall we discuss?'

What had got into Khalid? She could almost believe he was angry. All she'd done was stop him acting the part of smitten lover. She knew it was purely for public consumption, but still it came too close to her secret yearnings to be tolerable.

She reached for the golden goblet in front of her, swallowing the cool, rich cordial in an attempt to relieve her parched throat. She was aware of his eyes on her and felt clumsy, her movements jerky, her skin uncomfortably tight. Her hand shook as she put down the goblet.

'How long does the celebration last?' Out of nowhere a wave of tiredness hit her. The wedding ceremony had been surprisingly short, but the festivities had continued all day. It had taken hours simply to welcome all the guests. Then there'd been the various entertainments, including displays of horsemanship where Khalid himself had displayed a prowess that had brought her to her feet applauding.

'A few days.'

'Days?' Maggie couldn't imagine it. 'I don't think I have the stamina for it.'

His eyes gleamed but his face was serious as he said, 'We Shajehanis pride ourselves on our stamina.'

He was talking about the ability to feast and provide hospitality for days on end, not…anything else. Nevertheless, under his unwavering gaze, heat coloured her cheeks.

'Are we really expected to party for days?'

'No. Our customs have changed. Over the next few days there will be a range of festivities. The celebration tonight will continue until much later. I'm expected to attend most of it, but—' his gaze sharpened '—if you're tired, it will be quite acceptable for you to retire.'

'Really?' Suddenly the prospect of sleep was overwhelmingly tempting. A yawn rose in her throat and she stifled it hurriedly.

'Come.' Beside her Khalid rose, tall and imposing in his fine embroidered robes.

As she looked up at him a hush fell over the crowd. He held out his hand and she had no option but to place hers in his. It closed warm and vital around her fingers, drawing her inexorably from her seat till she stood before him. She trembled as his heat reached her, inviting her to lean close to his strong, perfect body. Instead she stood ramrod straight, her gaze fixed on his broad chest, rather than meet those dark eyes that she suspected saw too much.

He turned and led her from the raised dais. As he did so pandemonium broke out. Cheers and laughter and music.

Maggie faltered and looked questioningly at him.

'What's going on?'

She couldn't read his expression. It was set in severe lines yet even with his back to the lights she sensed his intense regard. His eyes glittered like black diamonds.

'They're encouraging me.' His lips quirked up then in what should have been a smile. 'They approve of the fact that I'm finally going to bed my new bride.'

CHAPTER EIGHT

KHALID led her through the scented gardens and into the palace.

Maggie racked her brain for small talk to fill the silence but nothing came. Her mouth was dry, her breathing agitated and her mind spinning. The touch of his hand on hers did that, the awareness of him close beside her.

And the fact that this was their wedding night and her handsome husband was leading her to bed.

Tension spiralled through her and an excitement she shouldn't be feeling. It wasn't meant to be this way. This was supposed to be a marriage of convenience. Yet now, feeling his dark lustrous gaze like a caress on her skin, Maggie acknowledged how desperately she wanted more.

She wanted her husband.

Her heart hammered against her ribs and she realised she was in an unfamiliar part of the palace.

'Where are we?' Was that husky voice hers?

Khalid opened ornate double doors and gestured for her to precede him. Warily she stepped into a wide vestibule. Intricately carved arches led off it and an exquisite old mural of a garden covered one wall.

'Our apartments.' His rich voice, low and close beside her, made her jump. 'We're in the heart of the old palace.'

'*Our* apartments?' Only those two words registered. 'But

I have my own rooms. I just moved in.' On the very day she'd agreed to marry him.

Khalid ushered her forward, brushing so close as he took her arm that she hurried to move. His proximity quickened her breathing, drew her skin tingling tight.

'That was before our wedding, Maggie. It would hardly be fitting now for us to live on separate sides of the palace. Now we will share a suite.'

Her breath stalled in her throat at his words.

They passed a vast, luxurious sitting room, then a smaller, more intimate parlour, till they came to another door. Its wood was decorated with a tracery of fine metal, like decorative vines.

They stopped and shock sizzled through her as he lifted her hand to his mouth, pressing his warm lips to her skin in a kiss that struck right to the core of her. Maggie stifled a sigh as her knees turned to jelly.

'You handled the formalities beautifully.' His voice, like black velvet ribbon, slid across her senses, evoking a longing for more, more of his words, his tender strength, more of *him*.

'Thank you.' Her voice was ridiculously husky because she couldn't catch her breath. Khalid's praise warmed her heart.

'I couldn't have done it without your aunt. Zeinab steered me through the preparations and the language lessons.' Maggie was babbling but she couldn't stop. 'And I've met some of her friends these past weeks so I knew some of the guests. That made it easier.'

'And yet it was you who played the part so magnificently.'

Played the part.

The words dropped between them, a reminder that this was all a sham.

Reality slammed into her. The bubbling excitement, the eager anticipation in her blood, died. She'd let herself be caught up in make-believe. He didn't want her.

As if on cue, Khalid released his hold. Instantly she missed his heat, the rippling energy of his nearness. She felt cold despite the balmy temperature. As if an icy hand had pushed her away.

He stepped back a single, telling pace and her heart contracted. That pace confirmed the cold, pragmatic truth about their marriage. The truth she'd secretly yearned to move beyond.

They were strangers. Married strangers. It was what she'd agreed to so it shouldn't have hurt so much.

'This is your room, Maggie. I hope you will be comfortable here.' He inclined his head in a courtly bow.

Khalid's words sounded stilted in his ears. Like a steward showing a stranger hospitality. Not a man with his new wife. But only by retreating into formality did he stand a chance of retaining any distance.

Damn it. This was not how he'd envisaged his wedding night. He clasped his hands so tight behind his back the restricted blood flow pained him. Better that than let his resolve crumble. If that happened he'd probably take her here, now, against the door, with all the pent up urgency of six weeks' anticipation.

Khalid shook with the force of wanting her.

He surveyed her confused eyes, her trembling mouth, the shadows of fatigue and emotion bruising her fair skin.

All day he'd resisted the truth, intent on his need to have her. He'd brushed aside Zeinab's concerns. Of course Maggie was nervous—what bride wasn't? As for being overwrought—no. Maggie was too grounded, too sensible for that. Even the doctor's guarded comments this evening, that Maggie was on the edge of exhaustion, hadn't swayed Khalid from his intention to make her his tonight.

'You look tired, little one. You need to rest.' He forced the words out.

He'd denied the truth right up until he'd led her from the wedding tent. Then he'd looked into her face, proud and tense and shadowed with weariness. He'd held her close and felt her tremble with exhaustion and nerves. She'd stumbled as her usual athletic grace had deserted her.

Only a brute would demand intimacy now, he acknowledged. He'd forgotten how overwhelming royal celebrations were for the uninitiated. To a woman isolated in a strange land, in the early, exhausting stages of pregnancy. How emotionally draining this must all be.

The doctor had stressed the need for rest to protect mother and baby. Khalid would have to wait. For tonight at least.

'Just ring the bell if you need anything.'

Her hazel eyes looked enormous as they met his.

'You won't be here?' Her voice was uneven. More proof that he was doing right. 'Don't you have to…stay for a while?' Her gaze shifted to a point near his collarbone. Thank goodness. When she looked at him like that it pared his resolve paper-thin.

'Won't it look odd if you return immediately?'

'Don't worry, Maggie. I won't go back to the feast straight away.' A long cold dip in the pool and some strenuous laps might temper the fever in his blood.

His smile was perfunctory. 'You go straight to bed and get some sleep.' He paused, only just stopping himself from touching her velvet skin, caressing her slender neck. 'Sleep well, little one.'

Maggie's shoulders slumped as she entered her new room. She barely took in the airy space, the canopied bed, the elegant furniture. A few tottering steps took her to a wide divan. She sank down, drawing her knees up to her chest, careless of her gown's priceless fabric.

Why was she upset? She'd known this marriage was just for their baby. That she and Khalid would never be a real couple. Yet the pain of rejection tore at her heart.

What had she expected? That he'd take one look at her in her finery and decide he wanted more from their marriage? Impossible!

Khalid's grim expression had spelled out precisely how un-attractive he found her. His heated look earlier, the one that had curled her toes with sexual anticipation, had been the product of her over-eager imagination. He'd virtually told her just now that she was haggard beneath the jewels and sumptuous clothes.

Her heart shrivelled. Suddenly this marriage in name only seemed a lifetime sentence.

Maggie woke in the late afternoon after falling asleep around dawn. She threw back the embroidered coverlet, then paused. Was he here? Waiting for her to wake? Did they have official duties today or were they expected to stay here, seeking privacy like normal newly-weds?

Fire seared her lungs at the images her unruly imagination conjured. Of Khalid, naked and stunningly aroused, lowering himself over her. Of the perfection of that moment when her body surrendered to indescribable pleasure. Of the warm clasp of his arms around her as he held her close in the after-math of the conflagration.

She bit down on her lip, wishing the memories weren't so vivid. She needed to forget instead of torturing herself with thoughts of what she couldn't have.

Khalid's strength, compassion and generosity, his determi-nation to do what was right by their child, all made him de-sirable. And that was without the bone-melting physical attraction she felt for him.

Twenty minutes later her nerves had settled but there was a hollow ache in her chest. The suite was empty. *Khalid wasn't here.*

He'd chosen to leave her alone the day after their wedding. For all the luxury of her surroundings she'd been dumped like an unwanted piece of luggage.

Her scent reached Khalid as he sat at his desk. Attar of roses. Not the cheap, pungent perfume tourists bought, but the true, sensual distillation that worked magic when heated on warm female flesh. On her it was pure eroticism.

Slowly he lifted his head. Desire crashed through him, stoking the deep-seated fire that had burned in his loins so long, ever since their night together. Every part of him hardened, muscles and sinews pulling tight.

She stood in the doorway, wearing an *abaya* of bronze shot through with green. Iridescent beads on the dress caught the light as she moved. His mouth dried to desert arid as she paced towards him. In this light, wearing what must be whisper-thin silk, it looked as if she was braless. The gentle sway of her breasts as she crossed the room held him fixated.

She didn't look tired anymore. And only a little nervous. Had she come to seduce him?

He smiled. Blood pooled hot and urgent in his groin.

Maggie's steps faltered, her eyes widened.

'Hello, Maggie.' The words emerged as a deep, satisfied rumble. She looked alert, refreshed, a bloom of colour in her cheeks. Satisfaction coiled inside him. And anticipation. Obviously his wife was feeling much better. Well enough for...

She stopped in front of the massive desk, crossing her arms as if to hide her breasts. But she was too late. He'd already spied the delectable points of her nipples pressing against the silk *abaya*. So she felt it too, the surge of hunger as their eyes met. The knowledge fuelled his need.

'Hello, Khalid.' Her voice was cool. 'I didn't hear you come in.'

'I just got back. You're feeling well?' he asked, needing to be sure. 'You've recovered from yesterday?'

'Yes.' Her brows knitted. 'I'm perfectly fine. I was just tired, that's all.'

'I'm glad to hear it.' The understatement of the year. 'Please—' he gestured to a chair '—take a seat.'

'No, thank you.' Her gaze darted around the room. 'But we need to talk. This pretence that we're married—'

He sat up bolt upright, instantly alert. 'It's no pretence.' His voice was rough with warning. 'The marriage is valid, Maggie. There's no going back.'

'I didn't mean it like that.' She pursed her lips and he read embarrassment there. But her eyes flashed defiantly and a jagged lightning strike of desire slammed into him.

'We need to discuss the ground rules,' she said, spreading her hands.

'Ground rules?'

'What you expect. How this is supposed to work on a day-to-day basis. We never talked about that.' She straightened her shoulders in a movement that thrust her small, perfect breasts towards him. He almost groaned aloud.

'Like today,' she continued, pacing restlessly. 'What was I supposed to do? Can I go out alone? I wasn't sure if you wanted me to keep the pretence that we were here…together.' She swallowed, her gaze sliding quickly away. 'But then you left me here alone so I assume it doesn't matter if people realise our marriage isn't normal.'

'Not normal?' Was that anger sizzling in his belly?

Her eyes met his and a blast of molten fire scorched him.

'Usually a bridegroom wants to spend time with his wife.' No mistaking the cutting edge to her words.

He stared. Did she truly believe he'd wanted to stay away?

'I did come to see you this afternoon. But you were still asleep. I thought it best not to wake you.'

He'd looked down at her curled in the centre of her vast bed and his libido had clawed like a wild thing, clamouring for release. Urging him to take what was his.

But he had an obligation to care for her. She had no one else. The fact that she'd slept so late only highlighted her fragility. Reluctantly, cursing his scruples, he'd returned to today's wedding celebrations, barely overcoming his frustration as he'd parried well-intentioned congratulations.

He'd only just returned to his rooms and tried to settle to

work, believing Maggie needed the rest of the day to recuperate. It seemed he'd been wrong.

Good. He'd waited long enough.

'If I'd known you were awake I'd have come back sooner.'

The shimmer of heat in his eyes disconcerted Maggie. It was like looking into the face of someone she knew and finding a stranger. A tremulous whisper of unease raced through her.

'Why did you come to see me?'

'Why does any man want to see his bride the day after their wedding?' His voice was a dangerous caress that warmed her blood and drew her breasts tight and full. His lips curved into a smile that seemed almost hungry. Her eyes widened and she backed a step, suddenly uncertain.

'Don't play games. Please.'

'You wanted to talk about ground rules.' Khalid's voice was a rich drawl. 'I agree. It's well past time for that.' The intensity of his stare held her taut and breathless as her heartbeat thudded, loud in her ears. Something had changed. Treacherous undercurrents swirled between them.

Deliberately his gaze moved, skating over her face, her bare neck, the rise and fall of her breasts. Silently she cursed the fact she hadn't bothered with a bra after her long soak in the bath. The rhythm of her breathing altered, now fast and shallow. A frisson of anxiety skated down her spine even as desire spiked in her bloodstream. She gasped and stepped back from the desk.

'Perhaps we could work the details out tomorrow. It's getting late.' Her words tumbled out in a rush. Maggie felt strangely vulnerable in this highly charged atmosphere.

'There's no need to wait until tomorrow,' he murmured.

In one lithe movement Khalid rose from his chair. At once the spacious room seemed to shrink, as if the walls pressed closer. Or maybe that was because her heart thudded so hard she couldn't catch her breath.

'There isn't?' Maggie watched him stride around the desk,

each movement slow and purposeful. She found herself turning so her back was to the desk and Khalid stood between her and the door.

The atavistic impulse to run and hide tensed her limbs. For the first time ever Khalid looked…dangerous. His easy, loose-limbed stance morphed into something much more aggressive. The expression in his eyes looked hungry, that baring of his teeth feral. She hardly recognised him. No sign now of the urbane, compassionate man she thought she knew.

Maggie blinked but the image of Khalid as a large, threatening, predatory male didn't shift.

Tremors of shock vibrated through her. And something else. A tiny thrill of excitement. She must be mad!

'No,' he said, his voice a deep rumble. 'We'll sort this out tonight.'

Her eyes were lustrous gold in the lamplight, shot with emerald fire. Khalid had never known any like them. Her chest rose and fell rapidly, her breasts thrusting in wanton invitation against the fabric. Her lips parted as her breaths shortened.

His body tensed to the point of pain as he prolonged the suspense of anticipation a moment more. He'd never been one to rush his pleasure.

And Maggie would be pure pleasure.

Tonight there was a fire in her, a vibrant energy that stoked his desire to smoking hot. The blaze in her eyes, that proud stance, her utterly sexy body were all magnificent.

He'd seen her brave, both in the horse ring and defying her physical weakness the night they'd met. Her stoicism, honesty and wry humour had instantly appealed. As had the way she'd battled an unhappy childhood and emerged strong yet still vulnerable and feminine.

'There's only one rule between us, Maggie. I am your husband and you are my wife.' Strange how satisfying the words were on his lips.

He closed in, backing her up against the desk till she had nowhere to go. Her eyes were stunned though she jutted her chin up. Was she fighting the force of need so powerful between them?

Her spirit, as much as her delectable body, made him hard with wanting.

'Really?' She was breathless. He liked that. The sound reminded him of her gasping out her pleasure the first time he'd taken his fill of her. It was a heady, erotic memory.

'Yes.' His voice was a growl. 'I will treat you as a man treats his wife.'

Her eyes grew huge and he watched her swallow convulsively.

He lowered his head, compelled to taste her again. She stiffened as his lips brushed the skin at the base of her neck. It was like rose-scented velvet, impossibly soft, decadently delicious.

For an instant her breasts slid against him before two feminine palms pushed at his chest. He nipped at her neck, a graze of teeth on sensitive flesh, and her hands faltered. He smiled as he inhaled her perfume and kissed his way up to the lobe of her ear.

'Khalid! What are you doing?'

'You don't like it?' He paused for a moment, lifting his mouth. She swayed a telltale fraction towards him in wordless protest at his withdrawal. Maggie's body knew what it wanted, even if she didn't.

'But this is surely what a bride expects of her husband.' He took pity on her, and himself, and kissed her neck, the angle of her jaw, the corner of her mouth. She groaned and shuddered against him as he drew her close.

He covered her mouth with his and plunged deep. The honey-sweet taste of her, the potent intimacy of that hungry kiss, sent spirals of heat exploding through his ravenous body. The feel of her slim curves pressing against him sent him into meltdown.

He needed to slow down. Quickly.

He slid his hands round her waist, feeling a kick of primitive satisfaction at the way they almost spanned her slim body. Then he lifted her up onto the desk, at the same time stepping in against her.

Urgently he reached higher, discovering to his delight he'd been right. No bra. He cupped her perfect breasts. They were warm, high and firm like delicious sun-ripened fruit. Her moan of delight vibrated inside his mouth as he squeezed. She spasmed in his hold.

He pulled back just enough to murmur against her lips, 'Sensitive?'

Wordlessly she nodded, her head falling back to leave her arched neck exposed. He slid his tongue along it, tasting musk. Ripples of pleasure coursed through her as he caressed her breasts through the thin fabric. The blood drew downwards in his body to pool heavily in his loins.

He bent his knees and took one breast in an open-mouthed kiss. The silk was no barrier to pleasure, becoming a slick second skin as he suckled hard, and she jerked in his arms, her whole body taut with ecstasy.

She was so responsive, so needy, so sensuous. He couldn't get enough of her. He wanted her *now*, and at the same time wanted to draw out the pleasure for both of them.

He wrapped an arm tight round her, pulling her hard against him. His mouth worked her soft flesh through the wet silk as he caressed her other breast. Gently he grazed his teeth across her breast in the tiniest nip.

She jolted in his arms. He could almost hear her heart pounding a frantic rhythm.

'Khalid. Please.' It was a choked gasp.

'Shh,' he soothed her as he straightened, his hands fastening on the fabric covering her thighs.

'We can't!' She shook her head, her eyes still closed.

Already the silk was bunched in his fists, her legs bare beneath his seeking hands.

'Of course we can.' He shoved her skirts up to the top of her legs. Her pale satiny thighs quivered beneath his palms. His need was urgent.

'You are my wife.' He hooked his fingers in her demure white lace underwear and tugged until she shimmied her hips, shifting her weight so that he could drag the fabric away.

'You're carrying my child.' His fingers probed the dark blonde triangle of hair at the juncture of her thighs, finding her satisfyingly slick and eager. This was what he wanted, the heady, physical pleasure she'd given him weeks ago then denied him all this time.

With one hand at her back he slid her towards him so she perched right on the edge of the desk, her legs falling further open as he insinuated his thighs between them. She was exactly where he wanted her.

His gaze roved her as he reached for the fastening of his trousers. Her eyes were slitted half closed against the pleasure that plumped her parted lips and drew her breath in short, hard pants. Her *abaya* bore the marks of his mouth, one nipple surrounded by an aureole of wet silk plastered to her breast. She looked glorious, wanton, ready.

His questing fingers probed her entrance, feeling the wet heat of her pleasure.

This time there'd be no need for protection, no barrier, since his seed was already securely planted inside her. The knowledge was supremely satisfying. And arousing. Possessiveness swept through him, so strong his knees trembled.

'Open your eyes, Maggie.'

Emerald light dazzled him from those golden depths. She reached up and curved her hands round his shoulders, tight, as if she was afraid to let go.

She looked bewildered by the force of their passion. Yet there was no shadow of protest from her. She felt it too, this prodigious, urgent need.

He positioned himself against her and slipped his hands beneath her legs. Her brow creased and belatedly he remembered this was new to her.

'Lift your legs.' It was a husky command, barely audible. His mouth dried when he felt her encircle him. He'd dreamed of this sweet ecstasy so often.

He splayed his hands over her hips, anchoring her as slowly, deliberately, he pushed inside.

She was just as he remembered, slick and hot and impossibly tight against his over-sensitive flesh. And the look of wonder on her face was sweet balm to his masculine ego. He rotated his hips just a little, watching the expressions of delight and astonishment flit across her face. Her fingers tightened, clawing through the fine linen at his shoulders. Pinpricks scored his flesh as her short nails dug in. Her breath was audible now, shallow pants that matched the rhythm of his pulse.

Carefully he withdrew, then abruptly surged forward, this time rewarded by a twitch of her pelvis as she lifted a fraction to meet him.

He smiled, though it was probably a rictus-hard grimace. Even that small effort to meet his thrust was enough to send him spinning almost out of control.

His wife was pure dynamite!

He'd never reached such a fever pitch of need so fast. Desperately he hung on to the remnants of his control. But it was no good. There'd be time for long, languorous lovemaking later, he assured himself. Right now it felt as if someone had lit a trail of gunpowder through his belly.

He shut his eyes, hoping to last just a few moments longer if he couldn't see her, so open and ready and generous. But in the darkness every sense concentrated on the feel of her all around him, delicious torture he couldn't withstand. The scent of her was in his nostrils, rose and earthy, feminine musk. The taste of her filled his mouth. The sound of her gasps of pleasure was all he heard over the rush of blood in his ears.

He thrust again and again. Felt her clench hard around him as her fingers clawed tighter.

Khalid opened his eyes as the darkness began to explode. He held her shocked gaze with his, watching the flush of sexual excitement flare across her throat, her cheeks.

His rhythm was steady now, smooth and deep, until she seemed to choke on a keening cry. Her muscles spasmed out of control and her desperate hands tugged him close.

He went willingly, nuzzling her warm silk hair, gathering her to him as the fiery heat rose and filled him. Flames exploded in his bloodstream and he was lost, juddering in violent completion that rocked them both.

When it was over he smiled wearily.

His plan for a convenient marriage had one definite benefit. Sex with his new wife was phenomenal.

Ruthlessly he squashed a niggle of unease in his subconscious. A sense that it was more than simple physical release that had made this coming together so powerful.

What more could there be?

CHAPTER NINE

KHALID slid the *abaya* off Maggie in one swift movement, then carried her to his bed. She felt perfect in his arms, a luscious bundle of warm femininity.

He didn't bother with lights for the moon lit the bedroom to a pale glow. Soon she was lying spread before him, naked and gloriously enticing. Her long legs and gentle curves were pure temptation.

His hunger rose again, unquenched. He frowned. He'd expected an easing of this urgency after their frantic coupling, but there'd been precious little respite. His climax had been a white-hot catharsis that should have left him sated. Yet the sight of her naked, like a delicacy offered for his personal enjoyment, had him ready for more.

His craving for her was marrow-deep. If he paused to consider the implications, he knew he wouldn't like them. He'd signed on for a convenient marriage, not one that stirred him to the very core.

She reached out a hand for the sheet as if to cover herself.

'No!' His voice was rough. Too rough. He saw her freeze, her eyes wide and luminous in the grey light.

'Leave it.'

Her breath shuddered out in a long sigh. Fascinated, he watched her breasts rise and fall, the nipples thrusting up at him. His hands itched to possess them.

Wordlessly he stripped off the rest of his clothes and let them fall. Then he climbed into the bed. Hastily she wriggled aside, thwarting his intention to blanket her body with his own. He'd revelled in the sensation of her impossibly soft skin, her yielding curves against him. He wanted that again. Now. But she was barely experienced, might even be tender. He swallowed his impatience.

Yet the reminder of her innocence merely fuelled his possessive hunger. There was undeniable satisfaction in realising all she knew of physical intimacy he'd taught her. His body clamoured at the prospect of initiating her into new pleasures.

Swallowing his frustration, Khalid propped himself up on one elbow and clamped his thigh over her restless legs. Immediately she stilled.

She needed time. Fine. He'd allow her that. But he had no intention of letting her hide herself from him. He let his hand settle on her collarbone and was rewarded with the rapid thud at her pulse-point, throbbing against his palm.

'You don't have to do that.' Her voice was so low he could barely hear it.

'Do what?' he said absently. He focused on the delicious curve of her flesh as he trawled the pads of his fingers down towards her breast.

Her hand closed hard over his, halting the movement. 'Touch me like that.' He heard her swallow. 'I didn't come to you for sex.'

'But it was good, wasn't it?' Satisfaction filled him. He turned over his hand and grasped hers, preventing her attempt to break his hold. He raised his eyes to her face. Even in the gloom he could read her pinched lips and shadowed eyes. Then she turned away, her mouth a flat line.

She was proud. Yet she was vulnerable too, unsure of herself. That made her prickly. She'd even had the temerity to turn down some of the gifts he'd planned to give her on their betrothal, saying they were too lavish, too expensive for her.

Most women he'd met had been fascinated by his family's legendary wealth. He'd forgotten there might be some who valued things other than money.

Shahina had been the same. Though born to a wealthy family, it wasn't luxury that had made her smile. It had been the things money couldn't purchase—friendship, shared joy, a mountain sunset, a baby's smile.

Khalid frowned. Despite their differing backgrounds, Maggie and Shahina had much in common. Not least their indomitable spirit. Shahina had lived with life-threatening illness, not letting it constrain her till the very end. Maggie had triumphed over the sort of childhood that, from the little he'd discovered, bordered on cruelty and neglect. Yet she faced the world with unique courage.

Strangely the comparison brought no guilt, no sense that he betrayed Shahina with this new marriage. To his surprise, Khalid felt instead a spreading glow of satisfaction. Of contentment.

Yes. He'd done the right thing. Marrying Maggie, bringing up their baby together, was best for them all.

He released her hand and slid his palm down to her proud, ripe breast. Instantly heat shot to his belly, his groin, and his fingers tightened possessively.

'I'll have your belongings moved in here tomorrow.'

There seemed little point in Maggie using the next room, even if there was a connecting door. They weren't in love, so it had seemed sensible to give them both a little space. But now she was here, her flesh warming his, he realised with a pang of surprise that he felt no desire at all for distance. He couldn't get enough of her.

He slid his leg higher across her thighs till he reached the heat of her most feminine place. She moved beneath him and a bolt of anticipation shot through him, pulling every muscle and tendon tight.

'No! Don't!' Her cry startled him.

She shoved his hand away from her breast with a force

that astounded him. 'There's no need to pretend with me, Khalid. Please.'

He scowled. 'What are you talking about?'

'I enjoyed making love with you.' The words tumbled out in a rush. 'It was…very nice. But now you've consummated the marriage and it's all legal. You don't have to…'

She stopped and chewed her lip. 'Could you move, please? I'd like to get up.'

'Not so fast.' Khalid couldn't believe what he was hearing. Very nice! His loving was *very nice*! Next she'd be giving him a score out of ten!

His head reeled as he stared down at her averted face, wishing now he'd turned on the lights so he could read her expression properly.

He pressed his leg down harder so she couldn't slide out from beneath him. After a few moments she subsided, lying still but for the agitated rise and fall of her breasts. She didn't look at him.

'You think what just happened, the sex we just shared—' he watched her flinch '—was a legal formality?' He didn't believe it. Couldn't believe it. Hadn't she been as moved as he'd been, by the stunning perfection of their love-making?

'Khalid, please—'

'No! It doesn't please me to release you.' His voice was harsh with anger but he couldn't prevent it. Anger with himself for having held back from her earlier? Or with her for being so blind?

Guilt clenched his innards. He'd taken no time tonight to reassure or persuade or even seduce her. He'd simply seen her, stalked her like a predator intent on its prey and taken what he'd wanted. Assumed she'd wanted it too.

'What happened between us has nothing to do with the law, Maggie.'

'Don't lie, Khalid.' Her head whipped around and he saw the bright glitter in her eyes. 'It has everything to do with it.

I know you don't want me. Not really. That first time you only stayed with me because I pleaded with you. You had no desire to see me again.'

He shook his head. He'd known Maggie hid emotional scars. He'd seen the evidence that first night. But he'd had no idea how deep they were.

'I was *there*! Remember?' Her voice rose, raw and throbbing with emotion. 'I saw the pity in your eyes, the reluctance. Well—' she put both hands on his imprisoning thigh and tried to shove him away '—we don't have to pretend anymore. There's no one but us here to see.'

'You think we had sex because I felt sorry for you? And then because I had to legitimise our marriage?' Even now he couldn't credit she was serious. Yet the evidence was there in her increasingly frantic attempts to free herself and the pain in her face.

'Do you really think we needed to consummate our marriage to make it legal when you're already pregnant with my baby?'

'I…I don't know.' She sounded confused.

'As for not wanting to see you again—it was you who left me, remember?' That still rankled. 'When I learned of Faruq's death I had to leave immediately. Otherwise you wouldn't have walked away so easily. As it was I had to wait for weeks till you could come to Shajehar.'

'Wait? You weren't waiting.' She shook her head, but her voice was less certain.

'Who do you think insisted on your coming here to work, Maggie?' His voice dropped low. 'We had unfinished business between us.'

'No!' It was a mere whisper of sound.

He took her chin in his hand and swung her round to face him fully. Lowered lids veiled her eyes but she was watching. He felt her gaze like hot ice on his flesh.

'No? Then how do you explain this?' He shifted closer,

pressing his burning hard shaft against her. The friction of soft feminine flesh against his rampant need was a taste of paradise.

Shock froze her features and her eyes bulged.

'I assumed…' She paused for the longest time, then swallowed convulsively. Her gaze slid from his. 'I thought you must have been thinking of someone else while we had sex.'

If it weren't so tragic this would be laughable. But right now Khalid felt more like breaking something. Fury swirled in his gut, edging his voice with a rough burr.

'Believe me, Maggie, I wasn't thinking of anyone but you. The reason I hesitated that first time was because I didn't want to take advantage of you when you'd been through some sort of trauma.'

'Oh.'

That was all she could say?

'Yes, oh. Believe it or not I have scruples about who I take to bed. Injured women who can't think straight aren't high on my list.'

The knowledge had haunted him ever since, that he'd taken advantage of her. He'd told himself she'd known what she was doing. But he'd never been able to shake that seed of doubt, especially when she'd run away.

'I slept with you because I desired you, Maggie. I still desire you.' He grasped her hand and pulled it down between their bodies, till she touched his turgid flesh. The sensation of those slender feminine fingers closing around him was sweet torment. A shudder vibrated through him and hot spears of flame danced behind his eyes.

'One thing you must learn to do, wife, is trust my word. I have already told you that I do not lie. Ever.'

The shocking reality of his arousal, hard, heavy and unbelievably exciting, stopped her thinking straight. The feel of his silky soft skin, his steely strength in her palm, was the most erotic sensation. Trembling, she snatched her hand away.

'But I…' *I what? I'm too gawky and angular, too unfeminine to be desirable? Too…unlovable?* Maggie bit her lip, her mind whirling.

'But nothing. You are my wife and I want you. Those are the facts.' He looked down at her, his breath warm on her already burning face. 'Do you want me, Maggie?'

Her breath stalled in her throat. How could he even ask? Hadn't she just melted in his arms, given herself up to the heady pleasure of his embrace out there, on his desk of all places? She'd been so needy, so abandoned, she'd been unable to pull back, even believing it wasn't *her* he really wanted in his arms. Her desperate hunger had swamped even her pride.

'I…' She swallowed the knot of emotion in her throat. 'I want you, Khalid. You must know that.' She had no pride left now. Nothing to protect herself.

Yet, even as the thought formed in her brain he lowered his face to hers, brushing her lips in the sweetest, most tender kiss imaginable. She sighed, feeling herself fall under his spell, uncaring of her surrender.

'I want you, Maggie. I desire you.' He pressed kisses to the corner of her mouth, her cheek, her jaw. 'You are sexy.' His teeth grazed the lobe of her ear. 'And beautiful.' He licked her neck and she shuddered. 'And every man at our wedding was jealous of my good fortune yesterday.'

His words melded into a deep husky purr as he rained kisses down her throat. Helplessly she arched against him, revelling in the whirlpool of sensations he created in her body and the glorious haze of well-being in her mind.

The words didn't stop. They flowed unceasing from his clever lips as he mouthed her flesh, slid down her body, caressing her. She was on overload, stunned by the sound of his husky, persuasive voice telling her again and again how beautiful she was, how desirable and how much he craved her. And all the while his mouth, his hands, his body touched her in ways that drowned out her doubts and fears and tugged her down, deeper into ecstasy.

'Khalid! Please, I...'

'Yes, Maggie. Don't hold back.' His words were muffled against her flesh, his breath hot, inciting flames of urgent sensation as he slid lower, to the place where heat pooled and swirled.

The press of his lips, the pulse of his tongue on that hypersensitive point was all it took to ignite her whole body in a roaring conflagration. It was instantaneous and indescribable.

When her mind returned to her body jolts of shivery delight still racked her, delicious aftershocks of pleasure. He slid higher, the heat of his body sheer erotic torture against her exquisitely sensitised flesh. Desire burgeoned anew.

'I love watching you come,' he murmured against her navel, his tongue flicking out to caress the spot. Maggie's breath seized at the edgy hunger hollowing her insides again. Her eyes widened as he tipped up his head and snared her with his glittering gaze.

'You're so beautiful. I want to watch you again.' His hand inched lower to her damp curls.

'No! Please, Khalid.' Desperate as she was for his touch, she needed more, far more. She ached for him.

His eyes held hers as the seconds stretched. The only sound was their breathing and the pound of blood in her ears. He was waiting.

'I want you, Khalid,' she whispered at last.

'And I want you, Maggie, my beautiful wife.'

He surged forward, positioning himself between her legs, and propped himself on muscled arms above her. The air was electric with anticipation as his heat surrounded her.

Heaven was in the deliberate glide of his erection against her slick folds. He was hard and heavy and potently virile. Even the brush of tickling hair on his legs against her sensitive inner thighs excited her.

'I need you, Maggie. Now.'

She looked up into the obsidian glint of his eyes and knew she wanted this, wanted him, more than anything. What she felt for her husband was stronger than pride, more potent than a lifetime's self-doubt, headier than anything that had gone before.

'Yes,' she gasped.

A second later he took her, fast and quick and urgent, with a breathless rhythm that confounded her lungs. But she didn't care. He wanted her, desired her. Just as she craved Khalid with every particle of her being.

The connection between them was so strong. Even when the climax broke upon her, he held her with his gaze and when the world splintered around her she wasn't alone. He was there too.

Together, beyond words, they shuddered out their release, their hoarse cries of ecstasy mingling in the darkness. And still that bond was unbroken between them.

At last, as the trembling eased and she dragged in a deep unfettered breath, Khalid pulled her over to lie sprawled across him, her cheek on his chest where she could hear the rapid tattoo of his heart.

'Never doubt that I desire you, Maggie.' His voice was rich and slow and deep, like the warm eddies of contentment swirling through her body.

His hand palmed her hair and her eyes fluttered closed. She gave herself up to sleep with a feeling of utter well-being such as she'd never known in all her life.

When Maggie woke the sun was high. Her lips curled in a secret smile as she remembered the pleasure, the intimacy, the tenderness she and Khalid had shared last night.

Her husband had given her such a gift. Not just the physical pleasure of his body, though that had been magnificent. A coil of desire twisted anew inside her at the recollection.

More than that, Khalid had looked at her and really seen. He'd somehow understood the uncertainty that plagued her, a girl who'd grown up without female role models. Whose tentative steps towards femininity had been ruthlessly crushed by a disapproving father who'd treated her like the son he'd wanted. A girl who had earned acceptance only by eschewing her femininity in a male realm.

The echo of Khalid's urgent voice, husky with need, telling her again and again how beautiful she was, how he desired her, filled her like warm sunshine. The way he'd looked at her, the unsteady rumble in his voice as she'd touched him, the way he'd loved her again and again through the night and above all his words, mellifluous then urgent then gasping, had convinced her as nothing else could.

Khalid found her desirable. He'd wanted her.

She'd been resigned to a marriage on paper only, for the sake of their child. She'd never expected the sort of caring he'd shown last night.

Surely he cared for her. He desired her. That in itself was miraculous. More than that, he'd taken the time to convince her, thoroughly and unequivocally, that he found her beautiful. He'd made her feel like a woman, precious, treasured and appreciated.

She breathed out on an unsteady sigh as she recalled his infinite patience and care last night.

There was desire, respect, tenderness. Was it possible that one day, perhaps, there might be even more?

Instantly she pushed the idea aside. She'd be happy with her new life here. She wouldn't chase after rainbows.

'A surprise? For me?' Maggie looked into Khalid's dark eyes and hoped he couldn't read her emotions.

After last night's loving she felt strangely vulnerable, as if in opening her body to her new husband she'd also let him into her mind and her heart. She'd never before trusted anyone enough for that.

'Yes, a surprise. Come on.' He ushered her out of the pavilion and through the palace grounds.

She kept up easily as he matched his long-legged stride to hers. This morning he wore traditional clothes again, the long robe and headscarf plain yet elegant, emphasising the lean, hard muscle of his powerful body. Maggie fought to keep her eyes on the path and not watch him avidly.

They skirted a courtyard, heady with the scent of blossom, through an archway tiled in turquoise and gilt, and into a familiar yard. The aromas of horse and hay filled the air and she frowned. She'd thought Khalid preferred her not to visit the stables now they were married.

'In here.' He gestured to a building she'd never entered. Smaller but no less luxurious than the racing stables where she'd worked.

He nodded to a stable hand and led the way to a roomy stall. Maggie looked in to find a pair of huge liquid dark eyes staring back at her. The Arab mare was gorgeous, alert and exquisite. She whickered into Maggie's outstretched hand and moved closer. Automatically Maggie smoothed her hand over her silky milk-pale coat, sizing her up.

'She's a honey,' Maggie murmured as she sidestepped to get a better view. 'May I go in?'

'Of course.'

'Was she bred here?' she asked as she ran her hand over the mare. 'She really is a beauty.'

'No, up in the mountains,' Khalid responded. 'She's only been here a few days.'

'You must be very proud of her.'

'You approve, then?'

'What's not to approve?' The mare was a dream, and, if her affectionate nuzzling was a true indication, good-tempered too. Maggie wished she could take her through her paces.

'You have a good eye,' she murmured. But that was expected. On their wedding day she'd seen him in a crowd of horsemen, all outstanding riders, yet Khalid had stood out among the throng. The sight of him—proud, capable and handsome—had set her heart singing. Of course he knew his horseflesh.

'I'm pleased you think so.' His voice was a warm caress. 'She's yours.'

'Sorry?' Maggie jerked round to meet his eyes. They gleamed with a heat that set her limbs quivering. Thoughts of last night and Khalid's passion, her own uninhibited responses, swamped her with edgy remembrance.

'Afraa is yours. My wedding gift to you.'

'Mine?' Maggie couldn't believe her ears. He was giving her the mare? This perfect horse was hers?

Her eyes widened as he nodded. 'Did I not say so?'

Maggie stared, dumbfounded. To be given any gift at all...but to be given such a precious thing. She blinked, opened her mouth to say something, then shut it. She had no words. The mare gently butted her with its head and she faltered back a step towards the wall, overcome by his generosity and by the way her heart filled at the gesture.

'Maggie?' Khalid was frowning, those sleek dark brows plunging down in a V. His voice sounded rough with concern. 'What's wrong?'

She shook her head, biting her lip as emotion twisted hard and sharp inside her. She couldn't remember ever receiving a present. Her father had treated birthdays and Christmas as ordinary work days on the farm. Perhaps there'd been gifts when she was younger, but those years were a shadowy blur.

She couldn't tell Khalid that. It sounded too pathetic.

'Nothing's wrong.' The words came out as a croak and she tried again. 'Thank you, Khalid. She's gorgeous.'

Maggie wished she could throw herself into his arms and kiss him, show him how much his generosity meant to her. But he made no move to approach and she hesitated, a lifetime's training holding her back.

'Afraa, did you say?'

He nodded, his gaze still fixed on her. 'Named for her white coat.'

'It's a lovely name,' she murmured, and took a step closer, wishing she could express adequately how much this meant to her. How he filled her heart with joy. 'A lovely horse. Thank you.'

She saw a flicker of expression on his face. A shadow of the heat that had flared in his eyes last night as he'd made love to her time and again, till she'd felt wanted and desirable. Instantly her insides melted.

'We will need to consult your doctor about riding while pregnant. But even if you need to wait until after the birth, she will be here, waiting for you.' He paused. 'I know it's difficult for you, Maggie, giving up your job, your home. Adapting to a new life. I want you to be happy here.'

Maggie rubbed her hand over Afraa's silky coat, emotion choking her at his words. He really did *care*. She was awed at the thought Afraa was hers. No gift could have meant more.

'I'm afraid I don't have a present for you,' she said, regretting that it hadn't even occurred to her.

Khalid held out his hand. When she placed her palm in his he drew her close. His heat, his warm scent, surrounded her and instantly her body responded, awaking into tremulous awareness.

'There's no need for a gift,' he murmured as he stroked his other hand lightly over her abdomen, his fingers splayed. It was a purely possessive gesture, like the kindling look she read in his eyes.

'You're carrying my child. What more could I want from you?' His words were smug with satisfaction. Male pride and ownership echoed in his tone and in the proprietorial glide of his hand over her body.

Maggie froze. There was no room for equivocation or misunderstanding. He made it abundantly clear there was nothing else she could give her husband. Nothing that he would want from her. Except sex, of course.

All that mattered to him was the baby.

It was like stepping out of summer sunshine into a glacial cave. Out of dazzling brightness into wintry darkness. A cold, hard knot of pain formed in her abdomen. So cold it iced her veins in a ripple of frost that sent a shiver across her skin.

She told herself it didn't matter. Their marriage was for the baby. If sex between them was passionate and exquisitely tender, that was a bonus. It was far more than she'd expected from their union.

Then why did it hurt so to be reminded that their marriage was simply pragmatic and convenient?

CHAPTER TEN

'TELL me about the school you went to, Maggie.'

Khalid watched her head shoot up from the page she was reading.

'Pardon?'

'Your school. I want you to tell me about it.'

He'd failed all evening to concentrate on the new plans for outreach education. His mind kept slipping to the woman on the other side of the sitting room and the change in her since she'd accepted his gift.

The mare had been a perfect wedding present, or so he'd thought. Maggie's eyes had glowed with delight, her face transformed by her rare beautiful smile. The impact had struck him deep in his chest, for a moment depriving him of oxygen.

Then inexplicably the light inside her had been extinguished.

It irked him that he had no idea why. One minute she'd been ecstatic. The next the shutters of reserve had slammed down, closing her off from him. And she'd stayed like that.

'Why do you want to hear about my school?' Her eyes were golden in the lamplight. They shimmered with doubt.

He got up from his desk, stretching. His eyes narrowed as he saw her furtive glance slip over him. He suppressed a satisfied smile. That was one area where he and Maggie connected—in their physical passion.

Her sexual response to him was deliciously enticing. A

mixture of innocence and erotic abandon that he found increasingly addictive.

He wanted to make love to her right there on the sofa. Make her come alive in his arms. His body throbbed with hungry anticipation.

Yet it wasn't Maggie's body he needed to win right now, but her mind, her guarded self.

He paced across to the sofa and sat beside her. Close enough to be conscious of her scent, her warmth, hear her soft, quick breathing.

'You were educated in the country, weren't you?' He gave her an easy smile. 'I'm working on a scheme to educate children in isolated areas. I'm interested to hear about the system where you grew up.'

Maggie shrugged and closed her equestrian magazine. 'It wasn't anything special. Just a small rural school.'

'How small? I've got options for building premises and for teachers who travel from place to place, going to the students.'

He saw a glint of interest in her expression and congratulated himself for hitting on the right topic. If he could get her talking, relaxing, he'd find a way to break through her reserve.

'I've never heard of travelling teachers before,' she said slowly. 'In the outback they have long-distance schooling, where students talk to their teachers on the radio and use the internet.'

Khalid nodded. 'That could be an option when we get proper internet coverage for the whole country.' He paused. 'What was your school like?'

He genuinely wanted to know. His curiosity about her grew by the day. Even after the physical intimacy they'd shared, there was so much he didn't know. For the first time in years he genuinely wanted to learn more about a woman. To understand her. The realisation intrigued him.

'Tiny, one classroom. A single teacher taught all the grades until students left for high school.'

'And it worked?'

'It was terrific.' She nodded and he caught a trace of en-thusiasm in her expression. It lit her face.

'Ah, I suspect you were an A-grade pupil.'

She shook her head. 'Unfortunately not.'

'You surprise me.' He'd already discovered Maggie to be intelligent and eager to learn. The dedication with which she'd pursued her language lessons impressed him.

She shrugged and looked down at the magazine in her hands. 'It was a long trek to school and sometimes I was needed on the farm instead.'

'Your father kept you home to work?' That surprised him, even though it wasn't uncommon in his country. 'I thought school was compulsory in Australia.'

'It is.' Her mouth twisted in a grim smile. 'My father made sure I went often enough that the authorities didn't have an excuse to intervene.'

'They might have thought you were playing truant by choice. It's not uncommon among teenagers.' But even as he spoke he responded to the pain in her voice.

Her head lifted abruptly and he read tension in her eyes. 'Oh, this started well before that. It began when I was eight.'

Eight! He tried to imagine Maggie at that age. Her deli-cate features, her slim frame. She'd have been a will-o'-the-wisp, a dainty creature. Fury sizzled in his blood that there'd been no one to stand up for her when she was so young and vulnerable.

'He should have been looking after you.' Outrage spilled the words from his lips. Her situation wasn't unique but that didn't stop the slow throb of anger. The intensity of his fury sideswiped him.

Again that tiny shrug of her stiff shoulders. 'He thought my duty was to him and to the property. He never understood that I wanted to do anything else.'

'Like train as a vet.' He remembered her saying that when they'd discussed her moving to Shajehar.

She nodded. 'It wouldn't have worked anyway. I didn't have time to study. Nor the money to go away to university.'

'You do now,' he murmured, reaching out and taking her hand. It was a gesture of compassion, intended to comfort her. Strange how the feel of her slender fingers in his sparked such pleasure, such satisfaction in him. Something about Maggie made him feel more…grounded, more complete than he had in a long time. Perhaps because it was so long since he'd felt personally responsible for anyone else.

Her eyes, wide and wondering, met his and a jolt of electricity sheared through him. What was this connection he felt with Maggie? It was more than just physical. He was unnerved by its potency, wary of this inexplicable force. But it was there, real and undeniable.

'You were serious? I really could study here?' Excitement coloured her voice. 'I didn't think you meant it. I assumed as your wife I couldn't have a career.'

'You couldn't take on a full-time load,' he said slowly, considering. 'You'd still have official duties.' And, in time, more children. He felt a burn of pleasurable anticipation at the idea of making more babies with his wife. 'But I don't see why you shouldn't train to be a vet if you really want to.'

'Khalid.' Her eyes shone bright and excited. 'That's wonderful. Thank you.' Her other hand closed round his, enveloping him with her warmth. His chest swelled at the sight of her smile, the awareness of her happiness.

So much pleasure at such a simple thing. Maggie was a unique woman. No wonder he'd come to…care for her. He lifted one hand to her cheek, slid it along the delicate beauty of her face.

'I'm glad to make you happy, little one. You deserve happiness.' He paused, the information she'd revealed still weighing on him. 'Perhaps it would have been better if your father hadn't raised you after your mother died. Weren't there other relatives to take you into their family?'

The smile froze on her face. 'Maggie?' He kept his voice mellow, not sharp. But a spike of anxiety shot through him.

'My mother didn't die,' she murmured at last. 'At least as far as I know.'

He palmed her cheek again and felt a tremor shake her as she drew in a jerky breath. He cursed the fact that he hadn't thought to question her earlier when she'd said there'd only been her father. He'd jumped to conclusions.

'What happened?'

Her gaze dipped, her shoulders rising in a shrug that was neither easy nor convincing. 'She left. Just walked out. When I was eight I came home one day and she'd gone.'

She'd left Maggie with that brute of a father.

Raw, aching emotion lay behind her staccato words. He could sense it welling inside her; taste its bitterness on his own tongue. Khalid felt helpless, faced with this anguish he could do nothing to assuage. An anguish that must have gnawed at her for years.

'I'm sorry, Maggie.' The words were inadequate, too little and too late. But he had to say them. It was doubtful she heard; she seemed focused on a distant place.

'I haven't heard from them since,' she whispered.

'Them?' What had he missed? 'Maggie? Who are you talking about?'

She looked up. There were no tears in her eyes. Yet the weary acceptance of pain he read there was more confronting than the sight of weeping. Instinctively he realised it was an acceptance she'd worked too long and hard to achieve. Tension knotted his stomach. He wished he could wipe away the hurt.

'When she left us my mother didn't go alone. She took Cassie, my little sister.' Maggie drew a deep, shuddering breath. 'But she didn't wait to take me too.'

'Maggie.' Khalid dragged her onto his lap, tucking her head beneath his chin. He hugged her close, as if he could protect her from the pain of the past. Slowly he rocked her, comforting her as he would a child, hoping the motion and the flow of husky words would help her find peace.

What this woman had been through. Rejected by her mother, neglected and used by her father. Forced to be strong and independent far too young. Khalid recalled her intriguing mix of forthrightness and self-doubt the night they'd met.

No wonder she'd agreed to marry him when she'd realised the security he could provide their child. The sort of security she'd never had.

He tugged her tighter against his thudding heart, inhaling the scent he'd become addicted to: roses and Maggie.

It was his duty to care for her.

But this didn't feel like duty. This was far more. Something gut-deep, something he couldn't put a name to. He couldn't bear to see her suffer.

'We will find them,' he vowed.

She shook her head. 'I don't think that's possible. I tried but they must have changed their name. I even hired an investigator when I could afford it.'

'Then we will hire a better one. No matter how long it takes we'll find them eventually.' He caressed her petal-soft cheek.

'Thank you, Khalid.' Her sigh was a shudder of pent-up pain that arrowed straight to his heart.

Maggie knew Khalid well enough to understand that his word was his bond. One day he'd find her lost family. She had no doubt about that. And the realisation brought an unexpected sense of peace.

He'd given her back her hope.

No matter how long the search took, she had faith now that it wouldn't be in vain, even if it took years.

Theirs might be only a marriage of convenience, but her new husband had just given her a precious commitment. One that had nothing to do with their child. His promise meant more than anything she'd ever received in her life.

Her throat tightened.

'Maggie? It will be all right.' His voice soothed.

'I know.' She pulled back in his arms and offered a shaky smile. 'I believe you.'

Dark eyes held hers and something powerful pulsed between them, warming her right through. 'Family is important,' he murmured. 'It's part of what makes us who we are.'

She nodded. 'You do understand.'

For most of her life she'd felt adrift, alone, despite being shackled by family obligation. If she could hear her mother's side of things, perhaps she could put the past behind her.

Though, here in Khalid's arms, she felt as if she'd already moved on with her life. As if she was ready for the future, whatever it held.

'What about you, Khalid? How did your family influence you?' She'd never broached any such personal issues before. But she'd just stripped her emotions bare. Surely she had a right to know him a little better.

Gently he stroked her cheek, brushed the hair from her face, and she almost purred aloud at the frisson of delight vibrating from his touch.

'I learned independence from my family.' His words, when they came, dragged her abruptly from a dreamy stupor.

'My father was supremely self-indulgent. More interested in his mistresses than his home life.'

Her heart contracted at the image he painted. Yet the proud tilt of Khalid's head told her he didn't seek sympathy.

'In a way that was fortunate. I was brought up by my mother who loved me unconditionally, and by my uncle Hussein, who taught me responsibility and duty, as well as a passion for Shajehar. When I was old enough, I went to boarding-school. I wasn't the heir, so my father had no expectations of me. He left me to my own devices.'

'It doesn't sound as if you minded.' Maggie wished her

father had been less controlling. She'd learned self-sufficiency but had rarely experienced the luxury of true independence.

Khalid shrugged. 'My older half-brother was the apple of my father's eye. He was indulged and spoiled. Never expected to work or take responsibility for his actions.'

Khalid's mouth curved into a smile that made her heart somersault. 'Instead of sitting here waiting to inherit, I was free to take my own path. An engineering degree in Britain. Business masters in the US, then development projects around the globe till I was ready to create a place for myself here.'

Maggie watched his face light with pleasure and enthusiasm. Clearly those years carving his own way had been a challenge, not a chore. 'Being left to your own devices hasn't held you back.'

He shook his head. 'We create our own future.'

His hand slipped down to rest possessively over her stomach, his warmth branding her. Yet this time, for reasons she didn't understand, Maggie wasn't upset by his proprietorial touch.

She stared into his heated gaze and felt a thrill of anticipation ripple through her. Her husband wanted her with a passion that never failed to amaze her.

She pressed her hand over his, enjoying the sensation of silky hair and sinewed strength under her palm and the heat of his hand imprinting on her belly.

Maybe, just maybe, over time they could build something far stronger than a merely convenient marriage.

CHAPTER ELEVEN

'IF YOU stand there, Your Highness, you'll be able to see the monitor.'

Instead of moving away, Khalid gave Maggie a reassuring smile and leaned close.

'All ready?' he murmured.

She nodded. 'I'm fine.'

She'd been on edge all morning, waiting for the ultrasound. Inevitably Khalid had picked up on her nervousness. She'd been touched by his decision not to leave and tackle the paperwork and petitioners and negotiations that usually filled his days. Instead he'd spent hours with her, showing her parts of the palace she'd never seen, exotic historic treasures, as well as places he'd haunted as a boy.

His tales of mischief and adventure and of long-ago Shajehani history had been a deliberate ploy to stop her dwelling on the nagging, irrational fear that the ultrasound might reveal something wrong with the baby.

'You'd better move so the poor woman can do her job,' she whispered.

He squeezed her hand. His reassurance warmed her and she smiled.

'I'm glad you're here.'

'I wouldn't miss it.'

She didn't doubt it. Their baby meant as much to him as it did to her. It was what bound them together.

The technician took her place beside Maggie as Khalid moved away.

'Now, I'll put this on ready for the ultrasound.' The technician smoothed gel over Maggie's abdomen and she flinched.

'Are you all right?'

'I'm fine.' Her lips curved up at Khalid's concern. 'It's just cold.' She could almost believe he was as nervous and excited as she.

'Here we are.' The technician ran the ultrasound device over Maggie's belly and she held her breath. For what seemed ages the screen showed shadowy images. Then...*there*. She stared, unable to believe her eyes as the screen showed the baby—real, alive, wonderful!

Her baby. Hers and Khalid's, alive inside her.

It was a miracle. Her body had confirmed in so many ways that she was carrying a child. But nothing, not even the couple of bouts of morning sickness, had made her pregnancy seem so real.

Tenderness filled her. Wonder, and a joy so profound it had to be shared.

'Khalid! Isn't it the most amazing thing you've ever seen?' Impulsively she turned to her husband, her hand stretched out instinctively towards him.

He didn't notice. His face was frozen as he stared at the screen. Tension vibrated off him in waves. What was he thinking?

'Khalid?' Her voice was a cracked whisper as anxiety coiled tight inside her. This time he heard. Slowly he blinked and turned his head, meeting her gaze with a look of such burning intensity that she trembled. He looked...different. Not like the man she'd got to know these past weeks.

His mouth curled in what ought to have been a smile. Yet somehow it lacked the reassurance of a few moments ago. He stepped close, his hand curving tightly round hers. As if he never intended to let go.

'Does the baby seem all right?' he asked abruptly. 'Is everything normal?'

'Yes, Your Highness. So far everything looks as it should.'

Khalid stared at monitor in awe, struck dumb by what he saw.

A baby. *His* baby. The breath sucked out from his lungs as shock held him rigid. Nothing had prepared him for the reality of seeing his child on the screen. Avidly his gaze traced the outline of its head, the curled body with knees up. The rapid throb of that little heart.

Emotion held Khalid's chest in a vice as he gazed at the miracle before him. The whispered conversation between Maggie and the technician was muted by the roar of blood in his ears.

Once he'd thought he'd never have a child. It had almost been a relief, knowing he wouldn't pass on any family traits. There was precious little from his father's family he'd want the next generation to inherit.

Shahina had been so eager for a baby. For *their* baby. It had been a cruel blow, learning she'd never be able to bear a child. His heart hammered as guilt speared him. The one thing he'd never been able to give the woman he loved. Now here he stood watching his unborn babe kicking in the womb. A child created by a single act of intimacy. A child who, statistically, shouldn't even have been conceived, given the precautions he'd taken.

A child he wanted with every fibre of his being.

Khalid's mouth stretched in a grimace of pain as emotions, confused, painful and exciting, swept him.

Automatically he tried to clamp a lid on them. He'd told himself for so long that there was no place for emotion in his life. After his initial white-hot grief eight years ago he'd survived by not having feelings. Not intimate, soul-deep feelings that threatened to unman him.

Not feelings like those evoked by the sight of his innocent, unborn child in Maggie's womb. By the sight of Maggie, tears of excitement in her eyes, as she shared the thrill of this new life they'd created.

Something squeezed painfully hard inside him. An unfamiliar sensation that scared the hell out of him.

His breath hissed between clenched teeth as he realised that with this child, this marriage, he'd inadvertently opened himself up to the sort of emotional commitment he'd eschewed for most of his adult life.

But there was no going back.

He wanted this child. He would cherish it, keep it and its mother safe. A fierce surge of possessiveness roared through him.

His hand tightened on Maggie's. He'd look after them both. Whatever it took. They were his.

Khalid's face was a stiff mask as he escorted Maggie back to their apartments. He looked like a man facing an unwanted reality.

A hollow feeling yawned in the pit of Maggie's belly. This morning's smiling companion had disappeared, replaced by a man she didn't know. A man of controlled, punctilious courtesy.

The memory of his searing look back at the clinic still made her heart race. That stare had ravaged her soul, filled her with doubt and confusion. She hadn't been able to read his thoughts, only his spiralling tension, the fact that he hadn't grinned in spontaneous delight at seeing their baby. He hadn't smiled at all. Something was wrong.

Was he regretting the baby? Resenting her?

She pursed her mouth to hide the ragged hurt tearing through her. She clasped her hands tight, holding the envelope with the ultrasound photo carefully between them.

It would be all right. Of course it would.

After seeing Khalid with children, Maggie knew he'd love their baby once it was born. He had a warm, caring nature. A man like that wouldn't be able to resist loving his own flesh and blood.

Maggie wasn't foolhardy enough to expect him to extend that love to include her. It was enough that he was kind and generous. An ardent lover. He'd be a wonderful father.

'After you.' He held open the door to their sitting room and stood aside, waiting for her to enter.

'Thank you.' She grimaced, hearing her stilted tone.

Silently she crossed the room, pausing before the antique silk-covered settees grouped cosily together.

'Do you need to lie down? You look tired.'

Maggie shrugged, thankful that was all he'd read in her face. Not the confusion or the pain that lay so close to the surface. 'I'm a little weary, but no more than usual.' She'd been lucky so far with an uneventful pregnancy.

'I'll leave you to rest in that case.' He sounded relieved. He stood several paces away, as if reluctant to get close. Cold shivered along her arms.

How different from this morning when he'd touched her so readily as he'd guided her through the old palace. That easy camaraderie had vanished. Did he regret their marriage? Regret their child? No, not that. He wanted their baby at least.

Suddenly Maggie realised how desperately she needed his strong arms about her. The reassurance of his embrace. She'd come to rely on that more and more. She'd taken comfort and strength from his generous warmth and physical tenderness. She rubbed her hands over her arms as a chill invaded her body.

'Are you all right?' His voice was sharp and she averted her face, not wanting to reveal the pain that held her taut.

She didn't know what had happened back there at the clinic. She just knew that something had changed. That once more she felt adrift and alone.

'Yes, of course.' She stepped away hurriedly, towards the book-lined end of the room where Khalid sometimes worked. 'I'll just put this picture somewhere safe.'

She found herself in front of the floor-to-ceiling bookshelves. She'd walked here at random, needing to get away from his acute gaze. Now she stood, staring blankly at the fine collection of books in English, Arabic and French. The rustle of paper reminded her of the envelope she clutched in her hands. The photo of their baby.

A shaft of pain lanced her chest. Suddenly she wanted nothing more than to be completely alone, away from the bitter-sweet temptation of Khalid's presence. She swung round towards the desk.

'Do you mind if I put it here for now?' She didn't look up or wait for his agreement. She gabbled on, needing to fill the silence. 'I'll get an album, a nice big one to put lots of baby photos in. But for now it'll be safe here where it can be kept flat.'

She dragged open the top drawer filled with pens, rulers, a calculator and various stationery equipment.

'Do you think I could find one at the souk? Zeinab said she'd take me there one day soon. Or would I need to go to a department store?' She pushed the drawer in and reached for the next one. This was better. Notepads and soft leather-bound books. The photo would be safe here.

Maggie lifted a book and placed the precious envelope beneath it. 'There, that's perfect. Tomorrow I'll buy an album.' She lifted her head and flashed a brief smile in his direction, vaguely noticing that he'd stopped on the other side of the desk.

At the same time she realised it wasn't a book she held but a large leather photo frame. Her fingers traced the padded outline of the frame and the glass protecting the picture. Automatically she turned it over in her hands. Khalid's abrupt movement, hurriedly stilled, snared her attention. She took in his hands, knotted in fists at his sides, and the heavy throb of his pulse at the base of his neck, visible even from here. His dark eyes were blank.

That non-expression scared her. Suddenly she knew she'd trespassed into private territory.

Anxiety whispered through her.

Slowly she lowered the frame into the open drawer, her eyes fixed on his. He didn't even blink. Maggie's pulse sped up. She felt as if she held something living, breathing and taboo in her hands. Or was her imagination working overtime? Khalid hadn't said anything. He just stood there…waiting.

Her hands went to the handle of the drawer and she began to slide it in. Still no reaction from Khalid.

See, she was imagining things. Maybe he was right and she was overtired. She'd been putting in so many extra hours on her language lessons and her visits with Zeinab to community centres. Maybe she'd been overdoing it, trying so hard to fit into this strange new world and find a place for herself here.

The thought died abruptly as her gaze lowered and she knew in an instant that she hadn't imagined a thing.

There was an audible hiss as she sucked in her breath.

Khalid looked so young. Impossibly young and handsome, like some glowing prince in a fairy tale. And that smile. It stopped the breath in her throat. She'd never seen him smile like that, with utter joy, as if he held the world in his hands.

Absently she reached down and stroked her fingertips over his face in the photo. The glass was cold beneath her touch.

He took a step towards her as she spoke.

'What was her name?'

Khalid halted abruptly an arm's length from her. She didn't look up. Instead her eyes were fixed on the face of the woman smiling up at him in the picture. Maggie had a sinking feeling that she knew exactly who the woman was. With her henna-decorated hands, her rich costume and familiar jewels, it wasn't hard to guess.

Maggie snatched her hand from the photo as if it might bite, bracing her arm instead on the edge of the desk.

'Her name was Shahina.' His tone was coolly blank. Instinctively Maggie understood it hid emotions too strong to share.

She looked down into the radiant faces, into the love that shone unmistakably in their eyes. It was there in the way they leaned together, in the shared intimacy captured in that moment even though they did no more than hold hands.

They looked beautiful, glorious.

Suddenly she felt worse than a fool for the stupid secret hopes she'd been unable to repress completely. The hopes of a real marriage one day. A fulfilling relationship. She felt a fraud, an imposter.

'She was a beautiful bride.' A raw ache filled Maggie.

'That photo was taken on our wedding day. Ten years ago.' His voice was clipped and unemotional, but he couldn't hide the pain that tinted his words.

Maggie heard a noise like the echo of a heavy metal door clanging shut, leaving her once more alone on the outside. Was it the thud of her heart? Had she imagined it?

It didn't matter. The truth was there, clear to see. Khalid had been utterly, vibrantly, unselfconsciously in love with his bride.

Maggie tasted the salt tang of blood as her teeth sank into her bottom lip. At least it stifled the burble of inappropriate laughter that threatened to spill out. How different her own wedding had been. She wondered if the guests had seen the difference, had known that their sheikh had married this time, not for love, but out of duty.

Of course they had. It must have been blatantly obvious.

How wrong she'd been, assuming it was disapproval she'd read in his expression when he'd said he no longer had a wife. He'd looked so furious she'd jumped to the conclusion there'd been a divorce. Now she realised his rigid control had been because she'd touched a raw nerve. The mention of his wife had evoked too many memories.

Finally she found her voice, though it was shaky. 'You must have been very young.'

'I was twenty. She was eighteen. But we'd known each other all our lives. We grew up together.'

They'd shared so much.

'She was very, very beautiful,' she whispered.

His first wife had been everything Maggie wasn't. Tiny, vivacious, lusciously curved, with sloe-dark eyes that sparkled, abundant black hair and perfect features. She was like a pretty doll, yet it was the utter happiness in her smile that made her so impossibly gorgeous.

Any woman would feel inferior to the lovely Shahina.

Jealousy stabbed her. Not for Shahina's exquisite looks, but because she had the one thing Maggie knew now she could never win for herself. Khalid's love.

Maggie had basked in the ecstasy of Khalid's solicitude, his easy companionship, his urgent passion. Only now did she acknowledge that wasn't enough. That, greedily, she wanted more.

Because she'd discovered she felt far too much for him. Because respect and companionship and sizzling sex showed her a glimpse of how life could be. If only Khalid's relationship with her were driven by his heart and not duty.

She slid the drawer completely closed and leaned forward, her grip on the desk white-knuckled. She'd seen enough. Her heart thudded painfully against her ribcage, so hard it must surely bruise.

'She was always full of life.' His words gave nothing away, but Maggie could feel the pain behind the words.

'What happened?' She didn't look up. Didn't want to meet his eyes and see the memories there.

Abruptly he moved, pacing in front of the desk, then stopping to stare out the window.

'She was asthmatic. Severely asthmatic. Her parents were told she might not survive into adulthood.'

Maggie's heart squeezed, knowing what was coming.

'Medication and a treatment plan kept the condition under

control. But she had an attack one day when we were far from the capital.' He paused and she heard him suck in a deep breath.

'It was so sudden. The medication did no good. She needed a hospital but we couldn't get her there in time. My father was entertaining VIPs and had commandeered even the medical emergency helicopters to take his guests on a desert picnic. By the time we diverted one to pick her up, it was too late.'

'I'm so sorry,' Maggie whispered, feeling the inadequacy of those words as she raised her head and took in the taut outline of Khalid's frame.

'It was a long time ago. Eight years.'

But not long enough to ease his grief. Now she understood why, despite his attentiveness, his consideration, Khalid had always seemed to hold a vital part of himself back.

Maggie swallowed down the salty, bitter taste of pain. Pain for the lovely Shahina, dead so early. Pain for Khalid who clearly had never got over the loss of his first wife. Pain for herself, the woman who could never fill Shahina's shoes. The woman who was destined always to be an inadequate surrogate in Khalid's life.

Despite his assurances, it must be incredibly difficult for him to take Maggie in his arms. To have her in his bed, his life, instead of the woman he'd loved.

When they were together, did he think of Shahina? Did the night-time darkness blanket the truth just enough so he could pretend it was Shahina he held, not Maggie?

A sob rocketed up in Maggie's throat and she clung to the desk, needing all her willpower to stifle it.

He never promised love. He's giving you all he can. You should be thankful for what you've got.

But this time it was too hard to accept. She didn't want to be his duty wife, she realised on a surge of defiant emotion. She wanted to fight for what she wanted, for Khalid. She wanted to win him for herself.

She loved him. Had fallen for the proud, honourable man

who'd given her tenderness, introduced her to pleasure, promised her security. Who'd married her because he'd felt he had to but who had made her happier than she'd ever been.

'Where are you going?' His voice was abrupt, jerking her out of her thoughts.

She paused in mid-step and turned just enough to send a vague glance in his direction, not daring to meet his gaze. Her feelings were too raw. She feared he'd read her as easily as a book.

'To the stables. I haven't seen Afraa all day. Besides, the children are due to visit.'

'I'd forgotten. I'll come with you.'

'But what about your work? You've already taken the whole morning off.' She was startled enough to meet his gaze head-on. It was like being sucked deep into a swirling tide. The blankness was gone from his eyes, replaced by a look she couldn't interpret. A look that scalded the blood beneath her skin and snagged her breath.

'The kingdom won't fall apart if I spend a day with my family.'

His family… Of course, he meant his cousin's children.

Maggie lifted her chin, hiding her hurt, as well as the inevitable, traitorous thrill of pleasure as he took her hand and drew her towards the door.

CHAPTER TWELVE

KHALID left his office and turned into a corridor, his steps slowing at the surprising sound of feminine laughter.

A door was ajar and he paused to look in. The room was full of women, like brightly coloured birds in their traditional finery. He knew from their costume that they'd travelled far from their home in the mountains.

He took in the group, clustered around vast trays of syrup pastries and steaming tea. His gaze came to rest on a figure in amber silk. Tendrils of desire snaked through him as he remembered clasping her swelling curves close last night while they shuddered through another mind-blowing climax together.

Maggie spoke in Arabic, careful but fluent.

'It's lucky for me you are so patient with my poor attempts to speak your language.'

There was another ripple of giggles, interspersed with praise for how quickly Her Highness had learned.

Khalid stared. He'd known Maggie's language skills had come on remarkably. The hours practising with her tutor were paying off. But he'd never heard her so confident.

'It's important for me to speak your language,' Maggie said. 'This is my home now. Besides, one day I want to go to university and I need to understand the lessons.'

The women's questions came thick and fast. Could a woman really study at university? Could anyone attend?

Maggie answered their questions with the help of the official at her side. She even mentioned the new scholarships for students from distant localities. The scholarships that she herself had suggested to Khalid only weeks before.

'So,' she went on, 'one day your children might study at university. But first they need to attend the school being built for them.'

There was a babble of conversation as the women discussed the reluctance of some of their menfolk to let their daughters attend classes.

Just then Maggie looked across the room and saw him. Colour rose in her cheeks and her lips formed a tempting pout of surprise that instantly ignited a lick of flame inside him. Other heads swivelled and the conversation died. Hastily he stepped away out of sight, knowing the women wouldn't be comfortable in his presence.

It was a shame to end the session. Maggie's informal chats had achieved far more than his official efforts to persuade remote villagers to support the new schools.

But what preoccupied him was the way Maggie's face had closed as soon as she'd seen him. That mask of reserve she'd perfected lately blanked out all trace of the vivacity he'd witnessed moments before.

With others she smiled and laughed. Never with him.

Khalid felt a surge of impatience. He was sick of being excluded, treated as a polite stranger except in bed. There she came alive, an uninhibited seductress in his arms. Though recently even there he'd had to persuade her into intimacy. Her earlier spontaneity had gone.

Nowadays she seemed absorbed in her work for his reforms. The reforms he'd thrown himself into more and more as their relationship grew increasingly strained, their conversation stilted and too careful.

Once he would have welcomed her restraint. The fact that

Maggie didn't cling. He'd been a loner so long, shunning emotional entanglements since Shahina.

But now…something had changed.

Since the day he'd seen the photo of himself and Shahina and realised the love they'd shared, though still real, was a faded memory.

Realised he was greedy enough, selfish enough, to want more than a memory to sustain him.

'Khalid.' Maggie sounded breathless as she joined him.

The rich fabric of her *abaya* skimmed burgeoning curves. Each day she grew more desirable. The muscles in his belly tightened. He couldn't get enough of her. The faint scent of roses and warm woman reached him. He took her hand before she could hide it away.

'Khalid?' She sounded nervous. Not pleased to see him.

Frowning, he led her along the wide hallway, back towards his offices.

'I didn't expect to see you in this part of the palace,' he murmured as he ushered her into his private suite and snicked the lock behind them.

Her glorious hazel-gold gaze widened, then darted away.

'Weren't you supposed to be resting?' he asked.

'I don't need to rest. Not that much, anyway.'

'You didn't get much sleep last night.'

To his delight a blush rose from her throat and tinted her cheekbones. Maggie's physical response to him was a perpetual pleasure.

She moved a few paces away, as if uncomfortable. By night she was his every erotic fantasy. But by day it was another story. Increasingly she was cool, composed, distant. Always busy, with her language lessons or the cultural and social activities devised by his aunt Zeinab.

Too busy for his liking, he realised. More and more he found himself wanting to share news with Maggie, see her reaction or simply have her close. It was disconcerting to discover how much he wanted to share with her. But always he held back. Ingrained habit acquired over eight long years had made him keep his distance and each day Maggie's formidable reserve grew more rigid. One seemed to feed off the other.

He watched her rub a palm down her lower back and stretch. The movement pulled the fabric of her dress taut over her proud breasts and ripe belly and instantly Khalid felt desire coil like a spring in his lower body. He'd always found Maggie's lissom body gorgeous, but there was something decadently luscious about her now she was so obviously pregnant. Carrying his growing baby.

Khalid's pulse quickened.

'Come.' He held out his hand. 'I have something to show you.' The feel of her hand resting in his pleased him. Such a little thing, but so right.

'What are you smiling about?' she asked warily.

'I was just thinking I could have saved a fortune by leaving all the consultation for the schools project to you and Zeinab. The input from your meetings has been invaluable.'

'Really? The women respond so well to Zeinab. They respect her and trust her.' A smile brightened Maggie's face before she hastily looked away. It bothered him that she could light up with enthusiasm for a public works project but not for her own husband.

'But my aunt wasn't there today.' Maggie had run the session alone and she'd done it brilliantly.

She shrugged, not meeting his eyes. 'The women were very polite.'

'Or perhaps they were thrilled to spend time alone with you,' he murmured. 'Did you consider that?'

She shook her head. 'What thrilled them is the chance to send their children to school.'

Khalid wished his wife would smile at him with even half the enthusiasm she felt for the welfare of strangers.

He was annoyed with himself. Could he possibly be jealous of his people? His own scheme?

'Here,' he said abruptly. 'I want you to see the latest plans. They just arrived.' Without waiting for an answer he tugged her to the meeting table, selecting a roll of plans he'd pored over earlier. He felt the resistance in her stiff body and kept her hand shackled in his.

'Look.' He spread them out. 'See how the architect has adapted the design for extra space? A nurse will attend a couple of days a week to trial a mother and baby clinic.'

'Really?' Avidly she leaned forward, planting her palms on the mahogany table. 'That was one of the suggestions we put forward. The women will be so excited. Where will this be built?'

Khalid answered her questions, pointing out the locations on a map of the provinces, torn between pleasure at her enthusiasm and chagrin that it was for a set of blueprints. He shut his eyes, revelling in the warm press of her body close to his and the rich earthy scent of woman that made his blood tingle.

He wanted his wife. Here. Now.

Khalid let his hands skim down her sides, circling back to rest on the taut, erotic curve of her *derrière*.

She froze, her body bent forward, arms braced on the vast table. 'Khalid?' Her voice was sharp. 'What are you doing?'

'I want you.' His voice betrayed the extremity of his need. He stepped close behind her, his body blanketing hers. He licked the sensitive spot behind her ear, then nuzzled her neck in an open-mouthed kiss.

'No! Not now.' Her voice ended on a gasp of sensual pleasure even as her body stiffened against his touch.

'Yes, now.'

'And you always get what you want, don't you?' The bitterness in her tone was new, pulling him up short. Was it possible she truly didn't want this? Disbelief slammed into him.

Surely she couldn't pretend this spark between them was one-sided. She'd never faked her desire for him!

He skimmed his hands over her breasts and felt her nipples pucker. Instantly his erection throbbed in response. He laved the sensitive spot behind her ear and felt her shake.

'Are you saying you don't want it too?'

'I…'

Shudders racked her as he bunched the silk of her dress in his fists, drawing it higher until he could slip one hand down, under the stretchy lace of her underwear, to follow the delicious contours of her backside.

'You…what, Maggie?' She tried to step to one side. Implacably he stopped her, simply by widening his stance so his legs surrounded hers. There was no way out.

'Tell me you don't want this, wife, and I will stop.'

He was hard with need. Harder, more aroused than he could ever remember being. He ached for her with a throbbing hunger that threatened his self-possession.

'Khalid, please, I…' Her words ended on a sigh as his hand slid possessively over the swollen curves that cradled their child and delved again beneath lace. He arrowed in on the pleasure point between her legs. A tremor shook her and he smiled as he nipped at her earlobe. Yes! In this at least she couldn't hold back from him.

With a groan of surrender she pushed her pelvis against his touch, just as he nudged her legs wider with his knee and let his erection surge up against her buttocks.

'Say it,' he demanded, his voice hoarse. 'Say you want me.'

'I…yes, Khalid. I want you.' It was a husky sigh of need.

He rewarded her with a gentle bite on that erotic zone below her ear, and the deliberately slow glide of his fingers against her clitoris.

'Someone could come in,' she gasped, but her hips were already rocking in an age old rhythm that told him all he needed to know about her arousal. The liquid heat sliding over his hand signalled a desire that matched his own. His pulse ratcheted up another notch.

She was his, all his. His wife, his lover. *His woman.*

He was determined to have all of her.

Khalid wrenched at his clothing, freeing himself so he could slip his erection against her soft, inviting curves as he tugged her underwear down, out of the way. His body shuddered in anticipation.

'No one will come in.' His voice was a stranger's, a strangled burr of lust.

He wanted Maggie so badly. So completely. It was more, even, than sex. This hunger for her was something primal, something he didn't understand. And it was growing more, not less, as time passed. He wanted to brand his possession of her in the most primitive way possible.

'It's broad daylight.' The words were a reedy thread of sound, a half-hearted protest. Even as she said it Maggie spread her legs, allowing him better access.

Khalid's smile of satisfaction was a grimace of tension. He positioned himself then slid slowly, forcefully, into her slick centre. With one hand he caressed her between her legs. The other he slid up, over her taut, round belly to the ripe swell of her breasts.

She cried out when he cupped her, rolling her nipple between his finger and thumb. Her whole body jerked with pleasure and he took advantage to thrust deeper inside.

'Why shouldn't I make love to my wife during the daytime?' He thrust aside the unspoken question at the back of his mind, the inexplicable matter of why he wanted her insatiably, why she was so important to him. For now it was enough to know he'd never desired a woman as he did Maggie.

He withdrew a fraction, then thrust again, further this time, each glorious centimetre a revelation in need and desire and ecstasy.

'Let me take you to paradise, Maggie.'

This time their loving was stronger, surer, deeper than anything he could remember. She'd got into his blood, his very soul and he was helpless to resist.

He didn't want to resist.

'Once more, my felicitations on your marriage. You've chosen well, my friend.'

Khalid followed King Osman's stare and spied Maggie chatting on the other side of the room with an executive of an international oil company. The company currently drilling on Shajehar's border with Osman's kingdom.

In the months since she'd come to Shajehar, Maggie had bloomed. She'd settled into her new role amazingly well, overcoming her diffidence as she grew in confidence. It had been like watching a beautiful rose open and blossom.

'Thank you, Osman. I appreciate your good wishes.'

Khalid's body tightened as he watched her. Maggie looked superb. At seven months pregnant she was more luscious than ever. The drape of shimmering fabric emphasised her perfect posture. She was elegant, eye-catching and far too sexy to be out in public.

He didn't miss the oil man's body language. He too was aware of Maggie as a desirable woman, though he was deferential.

Khalid had to stifle the primitive urge to pull her close or, better yet, immure her in the women's quarters of the old palace, as his ancestors would have done.

Maggie smiled with genuine warmth at something her companion said and jealousy bit into Khalid, bone-deep. How long since she'd smiled at him like that? He didn't want a stranger basking in those smiles she denied him. With each passing week the gulf between them yawned wider. She was slipping further from him each day, despite the intimacies they shared.

'No wonder you weren't interested in marrying my daughter,' Osman continued. 'Not when you'd discovered this lovely pearl.'

'Your daughter is a fine woman,' Khalid responded through gritted teeth. He hadn't missed the avaricious glitter in his companion's gaze, the knowing appreciation of a man who considered himself a connoisseur of women. 'I was honoured you should consider my brother's suggestion of a possible link between our families.'

And relieved when Osman had accepted with equanimity the news that Khalid had committed himself elsewhere.

'Ah, but my Fatin wouldn't have done for you. I see that now.'

Khalid repressed an impulse to steer Osman to the next room where he couldn't ogle Maggie. He didn't want any man looking at his wife like that. Especially not a lascivious old reprobate like Osman.

'I enjoyed a chat with your wife earlier,' Osman said. 'I found her to be a woman of sense. Very refreshing. She knows how to listen and when to speak up.' He cast a serious look at Khalid from under shaggy brows. 'You are a lucky man, my friend. Perhaps more than you know.'

The comment, at odds with Osman's usual preoccupation with physical beauty, surprised Khalid. He hadn't thought Osman so perceptive.

The other man was right. Khalid valued Maggie's common sense and quick mind. When it came to his reforms, her enthusiasm had overcome her diffidence. She'd helped him find perspective when barriers to change had seemed overwhelming.

'I couldn't agree more,' he said, watching her intently. 'I couldn't have chosen a better wife.'

Yet dissatisfaction gnawed at his belly. She was his helpmeet, the seductress in his bed and soon to be the mother of his child. But it wasn't enough. He wanted…more. He didn't want this distance between them.

Memories of the happiness, the closeness, he'd shared with

Shahina surfaced. To his amazement he realised *that* was what he wanted. A real marriage. A genuine relationship, not a convenient arrangement, hemmed in by the unspoken boundaries they'd both set.

Not a pale imitation of his first marriage, but something unique and special in its own right.

He thought of himself and Maggie, truly together. Man and wife in every sense of the word. For years he'd shied from anything that smacked of emotional commitment. Yet now, watching her move on to charm his aunt and uncle and a cluster of diplomats on the other side of the room, he understood that the little he had of her now would never satisfy him.

What would happen if he smashed through those no-go zones they'd erected? What if he opened himself totally to his wife? Would she, in turn, trust him with her innermost self, the woman she was at heart?

Suddenly he knew an overwhelming need to find out.

I can't do this anymore. I just can't.

Maggie's face ached from an evening of polite smiles. But that was nothing to the pain cramping her chest, the anguish of knowing she couldn't go on like this.

She listened to King Osman make his farewells to Khalid, the sound of their conversation washing over her.

She'd felt Khalid's gaze on her all through the reception, like a stroke of flame on her vulnerable skin. She'd seen the speculative look in his eye, the flare of heat, and felt a traitorous answering spark deep inside.

But sex wasn't enough anymore.

For months she'd done her best. She'd accepted what fate had handed her—a loveless marriage. She'd tried so hard to fit in even though she'd finally understood that Khalid could never reciprocate her feelings. He was still in love with Shahina.

Maggie couldn't compete with a ghost. She was too weary

to keep trying. Second-best wasn't enough for her anymore. Desire without love was, she'd learned, an empty sham.

'Come, Maggie.' Khalid's voice was rich and warm in her ear. He slid her arm through his and pulled her close. 'Time for bed.'

Instantly her treacherous body leapt at the promise in his tone, in the heat of his powerful body against hers. She looked around to see the elegant reception room deserted but for the servants. Osman had left for his guest suite.

It wasn't far to their apartments, but every step was torment. The heaven of being held close by the man she loved, the man who woke her senses to shivering awareness just with his proximity. The hell of knowing she couldn't bear this farce of intimacy any longer.

Each caress, each tender word tore her apart, for they meant nothing. Nothing more than that he found her a convenient companion. He'd never *love* her.

She shuddered to a halt just inside their sitting room and reefed her arm from his, barely noticing his look of surprise.

She deserved more from marriage. If she couldn't have a real marriage, surely she had the right to protect her sanity and her self-respect. She needed to get out of this dead-end relationship.

'Maggie? What's wrong?'

She looked up at the man who'd held himself carefully aloof from her all evening as protocol required. No matter how she pleased him in bed, no matter how hard she worked to fit into his world, he would always be just that. Aloof.

Was that how it had been between her parents? Love on one side and not on the other? Was that what had driven them apart?

Memories of the intimacies she and Khalid had shared made her insides churn. She'd sold herself to him. For security and support for her baby. For the vain hope that love might grow from physical desire.

No more. It was time she stood on her own two feet. For as long as she put up with this arrangement she doomed herself to unhappiness.

'I'm going to bed.' Her voice sounded incredibly calm. But then, now her decision was made, she felt strangely free of the emotions that had racked her for so long.

'Precisely what I had in mind, *habibti*.'

He reached for her and she stepped back a pace. That casual endearment stung like a slap to the face. No doubt he'd used it with the countless women who'd satisfied his physical needs since Shahina. Maggie was no one special.

A gaping hollow opened inside her. A cold, cruel vacuum where once there'd been excitement and hope.

How could a woman so big with a baby feel suddenly so empty inside?

'No, not that.' She saw his expression change, settling into one of cool query. He wasn't used to being denied. Yet she found no pleasure in denying him, just a weary resolution. 'I want to sleep.'

'It's been a long evening.' Even now the deep timbre of his voice made her yearn for what she shouldn't want. 'Perhaps you'd like a bath first?'

And perhaps a little seduction in the scented, soapy water?

'No.' How often had Khalid seduced her in that decadently large bath? She drew in a deep breath and faced him squarely. 'I want to go straight to sleep. I'll use the second bedroom.'

Khalid's eyebrows shot up. 'There's no need for that.' Haughty reproach laced his tone. 'I respect your need for rest. I won't bother you tonight.'

Maggie traced his proud, forbidding features with her gaze and felt the inevitable kick of desire deep inside. It would always be the same, she feared.

Quickly she shook her head. 'I want to sleep alone. Permanently.'

Khalid loomed before her, a force larger than life, his features hewn into a look of arrogant disbelief. The only signs of life were the burning intensity of his jet-dark eyes as they roved her and his flaring nostrils. Then she looked down and saw the way his hands bunched into fists, white-knuckled with sinewed tension.

Once she might have been daunted by the sight. But it didn't faze her. She felt walled off from emotion in a bubble of nothingness.

'If my love-making causes you discomfort now the baby's so big you should have told me.' Outrage vibrated in his voice. 'I won't force myself on you. I'm not a selfish ogre.'

No, Khalid was a decent man. But their relationship destroyed her, sucking her soul from her till she felt hollow.

'It's not the baby, Khalid. It's me. I don't want sex with you.' *Liar*, screamed a voice inside her. *You'll always crave him*!

Yet having only that small part of him was killing her. Their bodies so attuned but their hearts…

His eyes narrowed as if he'd heard it too, the telltale voice of her needier self.

'I don't want *you*,' she blurted out before she could change her mind. 'I can't continue on with this marriage.'

'You want to leave me?' The words erupted as a barely muted roar. But at least he hadn't closed the yawning chasm between them and yanked her into his arms.

Khalid stared, dumbfounded. He'd sensed her slipping away from him but he'd never guessed it could go this far! Nothing had prepared him. It was impossible she no longer wanted him. He knew in his bones that she lied about that.

'You can't be serious!' She belonged to him. He would never release her.

'I've never been more serious about anything in my life.' Her calm, colourless tone, those almost-blank eyes, convinced him as nothing else could. Maggie wasn't speaking in the heat of the moment. She was in deadly earnest.

A blade of pain sliced through his chest. He braced his feet wider, rocked unsteady by the force of the blow.

Pride and anger surged to the surface.

'You forget, *my wife*, that we're married.' He took a pace forward, bringing him up against her. Part of him urged action: to haul her into his embrace and seduce her with his kisses, his body, her own need for him, till she recanted this nonsense. But pride, or perhaps sense, warned that seduction wasn't the answer.

'No one divorces in the royal house of Shajehar. You are mine and you will stay mine.' His heart thumped a racing, heavy beat that muted his words. 'I will not let you leave.'

Her eyes widened as she stared up at him, but not by so much as a quiver did her body reveal any weakening. She stood strong, determined and quietly defiant. Her composure was eerie, especially given the adrenalin pumping through his bloodstream, the shock tightening every nerve ready for action.

'I don't intend to leave Shajehar. I know what I signed on for and I know there's no easy escape.'

Outrage scorched his soul at her words. And something more. Something that felt like hurt.

Signed on for!

She made their marriage sound like a burdensome duty. Hadn't he given her a place in his world, a place where she was respected and valued, able to contribute? Hadn't he given her wealth, jewels and consequence? A secure future for her and her baby? Hadn't he pleasured her and satisfied her times beyond count?

He couldn't believe she didn't want him. Sometimes he'd even fancied that she felt far more for him than she wanted him to know. Or was that male pride talking?

'So tell me. What is it you do want?'

Her eyelids flickered, then she met his gaze steadily. 'I want space. Distance. I'll still be your wife as far as the world is concerned. But I don't want us to live as man and wife. We'll bring up our child together as agreed. I'll fulfil my duties as a member of the royal family, but…'

'Not in the marriage bed.' The bitterness in Khalid's mouth made him grimace.

She said nothing, just stared up at him with those enormous eyes. Her face was pale and lovely and strained. For the first time he noticed she'd used more make-up than usual. Were those shadows under her eyes? Lines of strain bracketing her mouth?

He looked down to her hands splayed over her belly.

Did she think she needed to protect their child from her husband's fury? The sickening thought made him step back a pace, his chest heaving at the impossible idea.

'Why, Maggie?'

She was silent for so long his nerves stretched to snapping point. Finally she opened her mouth.

'It was never a real marriage, Khalid. Ours is simply a convenient marriage. I want us to stick to that.' She paused and swallowed. 'It's taken a long time but I've discovered I don't want to be intimate with a man when there's no love involved.'

CHAPTER THIRTEEN

'How far till we get there?'

Khalid darted a look at Maggie, checking for signs of fatigue before turning back to the road. She sat straight, hands clasped in her lap. The rough mountain road didn't seem to bother her.

'Not far as the crow flies, but another twenty minutes by road.'

Silence. Their conversation, as usual these days, was brief and stilted.

Was he doing right, acquiescing even briefly to her demand for distance? He wished he knew for sure.

Two days ago when he'd looked into her preternaturally calm face as she'd announced she didn't want him or their marriage, she'd been devoid of emotion. Like a lifeless doll. Or a woman under such incredible strain that she'd shut down emotionally.

That scared Khalid more than anything she'd said. Scared him so much he'd ignored his instinctive need to shatter her sang-froid and prove she lied when she said she no longer wanted him.

I don't want to be intimate with a man when there's no love involved. The words had seared themselves into his brain cells to be replayed again and again.

Love hadn't been part of the bargain. But now, knowing she didn't love him, he felt an ache deep inside. An emptiness.

Only her vulnerability kept strong his resolve to allow her time to adjust.

Maggie had enough to cope with. Was it any wonder she'd been overwrought? Pregnancy hormones. The stress of adjusting to a new life in a new country. The onerous pressures of royal duty and protocol. Physical exhaustion at the strain the baby placed on her body. Fear of the unknown. Grief for the past she'd left behind. The demands he'd put on her, with his incessant hunger for her touch and her warm, luscious body.

He had to give her time. By the time the baby was born things would be different. He'd make sure of it.

'What did you think of the village school?'

'Marvellous!' He heard the thread of excitement in the single word and suppressed annoyance that she was so enthusiastic about a temporary tent school yet dismissive of him.

'You were a hit,' he murmured. 'The children loved you and the parents all approved.'

Khalid had watched the little ones clustering around her as she rocked a toddler on her lap and listened to the juvenile chatter. He'd wanted to be with her, not talking to the village head man.

Primal heat had shot through him at the sight of Maggie cradling a child. Soon she'd have their child to nurse. Satisfaction filled him. And trepidation.

No! By then their marriage would be on track. Everything would be settled. He just needed to curb his impatience.

'Tell me what the women thought of the new school,' he prompted.

He wanted to hear her voice, especially now, he realised as the treacherous road turned into a series of hairpin bends and grim memory surfaced. Tension knotted his stomach and his hands grew clammy on the wheel.

He remembered bringing another woman this way years ago. Driving her up this road as they laughed together.

But Shahina hadn't come down alive.

The sun shone high as they crossed the narrow bridge spanning a chasm that separated the castle from the rest of the mountain spur. It was a grim fortress, squat and foreboding, rising out of sheer rock to command the valley far below and the route over the mountains above.

Maggie barely took in the massive metal-studded wooden doors, the walls, thicker than a man's shoulders, and the iron grille-work in the few windows facing the mountain.

Her thoughts focused on the man beside her, whose gentle support—an arm around her back and another at her elbow—was the most exquisite torture. His tone was solicitous, his pace shortening to her pregnant gait.

Anyone seeing them would believe their prince really cared for his wife. But they'd be wrong. The knowledge was a fathomless black well of despair inside her.

He cared, all right, cared that his precious baby was protected. But as for her, she was a necessary burden, an incubator to carry the child till it entered the world.

Unfortunately the emotionless limbo that had given her strength and cushioned her from pain had faded. Even the fact that Khalid had reluctantly respected her wishes to sleep in separate rooms brought no comfort.

She shivered and his arm tightened.

'Her Highness needs tea, in the small salon,' he said.

The steward who welcomed them bowed and turned to do his master's bidding. Maggie moved mechanically, letting Khalid lead her.

'Here. You'll feel better when you have your tea and something to eat.'

Maggie's lips pulled tight in a grimace. She doubted anything would make her feel better ever again. She subsided into the cushioned chair he held out for her, letting her weary, heavy body sink back. Every bone ached. She felt old beyond her years and tired, so very tired.

'Maggie?' She turned her head slightly at the sound of his voice, deeper, more resonant than usual. But she didn't meet his gaze as he hunkered down before her, pulling her limp hand into his. 'Are you all right?'

She blinked; her stupid imagination tinted his voice with a husky concern she knew wasn't real.

She sat up straighter. 'Yes, thank you. But that tea will be nice,' she lied. The idea of anything on her stomach, even liquid, made bile rise in her throat.

Silence stretched. With each second the distance between them drew wider and more impassable.

Deliberately she turned her head to the huge windows looking out across the network of valleys below. 'The view is spectacular.'

He said nothing for a moment then, abruptly, he stood and tucked her hand in her lap. 'On a fine day you can see for hundreds of kilometres.'

Cloud had curtained the horizon since they'd arrived on their provincial visit. She wondered if he'd ever bring her here again to see it on a fine day.

'I have some business to attend to,' he murmured. 'In the meantime enjoy your refreshments. I'll be back in time to take you to visit the next village.'

Then he was gone and she was left in the empty luxury of the enormous sitting room, its divans covered in massed silk cushions, its floor bright with jewel-coloured antique rugs. Their entourage was no doubt filling the old fortress to bursting point and yet she could easily imagine she was the only one here.

An hour later she was still alone. The castle steward himself brought a second tray of tea, steaming, sweet and fragrant. The aroma curdled her stomach and she rose from her chair on a surge of sudden energy. It was time to go.

It didn't matter that she was heartsick and listless. Or that Khalid insisted on driving her and she didn't want to be cooped up in a vehicle with him. The villagers were expecting her and she wouldn't let them down.

Besides, if she sat here any longer, dwelling on the emotional stalemate her marriage had become, she'd go mad.

'Where is my husband?' She turned to the steward who looked surprised at the simple question.

'His Highness is conferring with Lord Hussein.'

Good. Khalid's uncle was a reasonable man; he wouldn't mind being interrupted.

'Where are they? I need to speak with my husband,' she added when the steward hesitated.

His eyes slid from hers and he pursed his lips.

'It is an urgent matter.'

'They are in Lady Shahina's garden,' he said quickly.

The chill that had been confined to her heart crackled now through her whole body, like icy frost settling on a winter's morning. Shahina's garden. That was where her husband chose to conduct his important business?

Maggie nodded briskly. 'You can show me the way.' She headed for the door and he was forced to accompany her. As they made their way along a vaulted stone corridor she asked casually, 'Did Lady Shahina plant this garden?'

'No, Highness.' She heard the discomfort in his voice and almost felt sorry for him. 'Your Lord had it made after she…'

'I see. After she died.' A memorial garden, then.

Her husband had taken refuge in the place dedicated to the memory of his lost love.

See? She'd been right to stand up for herself. He'd never love her while Shahina held his heart. Far better to distance herself from Khalid than pine for what could never be. But that didn't stop the pain winding round her heart like a constricting vine.

She faltered in an arched doorway, her hand going protectively to her belly where their baby stretched and kicked.

'Highness? Are you all right?'

She straightened. 'Yes, thank you. Is it much further?'

He shook his head. 'Straight ahead, through the door into the first courtyard, then right at the next doorway.'

'Thank you.' Maggie glued a perfunctory smile on her face. 'I'll find my own way from here. I'm sure you have a lot to organise with so many guests.'

She waited till he left, till the corridor was whisper-quiet, before continuing.

The flagstones were warm beneath her feet when the scent assailed her. Damask roses and jasmine and a bounteous mix of other perfumes. In her pregnant state, the voluptuous riot of scents cloyed. Maggie paused at the arched doorway into the walled garden, one hand outstretched to the stone wall as she tried to stifle the queasiness in her stomach.

It was a moment before she realised there were voices. At the sound of Khalid's low tones she stole a step closer to the doorway. She stared at the two men on the other side of the garden.

'Don't you think you should talk to Maggie?' said Khalid's uncle.

'I know what's best, Hussein. You don't understand—'

'I understand, Khalid. Remember I saw you and Shahina together. I see you now with Maggie. I know how you feel.'

'That's not the point. I know what I'm doing.'

Maggie sagged against the doorway as her knees buckled. Khalid sounded so savage, so desperate.

'She isn't Shahina,' Hussein said in a low voice. 'You need to remember that.'

'Don't you think I know that?' Khalid's tone was brusque, rising on harsh emotion. 'Every time I see her, touch her, I know the difference.' There was intrinsic violence in his gesture as he flung out his arm, in the abrupt way he turned and paced, that spoke more loudly of his feelings than even his terse words.

'I feel it *here*.' He thumped his chest so hard it was a wonder Maggie couldn't hear it resonate. Maybe her gasp of anguish drowned out the sound. She reeled back as if he'd slammed his fist against her, robbing her of air.

'Have you told her how you feel? You have to take the time to explain to her.'

But Maggie didn't need explanations. She stumbled back from the doorway, so distraught she barely noticed when her ice-blue scarf snagged on a climbing rose.

Khalid had made himself abundantly clear. She couldn't face any more.

The desolation in his voice left no room for doubt. The confirmation that he missed his first, beloved wife so much tore what was left of her heart to shredded ribbons.

She groped her way out of the courtyard, one hand outstretched to the stone wall, the other supporting her heaving belly. She had to get away, somewhere she could breathe. Even here in the courtyard the air was too close and thick, choking her.

She stumbled through a threshold and found herself in the entrance yard. Ranks of four-wheel drives were lined up where once there'd been battle horses.

Maggie looked at her watch. She'd need to leave now if she wasn't to disappoint the locals who'd so shyly offered their hospitality. Khalid...her heart drummed painfully...Khalid had clearly forgotten the appointment. Should she search for someone else to accompany her? The last thing she wanted was a minder.

Apparently the village was an easy fifteen-minute drive. It was broad daylight and she was used to driving on gravel roads, or she had been till she'd become a royal princess.

Khalid would know where she'd gone. He wouldn't worry.

She pushed back her sagging shoulders. She would *not* hide in a corner and fret over what she couldn't change. Wasn't that what she'd promised herself when she'd confronted Khalid? She had to move on with her life.

She made for the vehicle closest to the open gate. Three minutes later the engine roared into life. Without a backward glance she drove out, across the narrow bridge and onto the mountain road.

She'd driven four kilometres when she saw the turn-off Khalid had pointed out. She turned into it, glad to escape the claustrophobic confines of the castle that was Khalid and Shahina's. Where Maggie would always be an intruder.

Work had always been a necessity and a solace. That was what she needed. To focus on her baby and her work with the Shajehani women. If she kept busy enough maybe one day the pain of unrequited love would ease. Then she could think of Khalid and not have tears blur her vision and choke her breathing.

She rounded a blind curve and her heart jolted as a couple of goats raced across the road metres away. She slammed on the brakes, then cursed as the wheels locked and the vehicle slid sideways in the gravel. Her reflexes were slow and her hands slipped on the steering wheel as she tried to turn into the skid.

The seconds stretched out impossibly as the vehicle headed for the edge. A deep gutter and a cutting of sheer rock loomed beside her as she struggled with the wheel.

It was impossible.

The impact threw her forward with a jolt that shook her teeth and bruised her body. She curled her arms around her belly, trying desperately to protect her baby.

There was a terrible, blood-curdling screech, banshee-loud, as metal scraped on rock. The vehicle tipped half over in the ditch and kept sliding. Maggie barely noticed. She'd knocked her head on the initial impact.

At last the ear-splitting shriek of tortured metal ceased. The vehicle thudded to a halt at a forty-five-degree angle against a ridge of solid rock.

Eventually she summoned the energy to reach up and switch off the ignition. The only sounds were the tick, tick of hot metal and her rough panting breaths as she fought pain and the dizzying tug of unconsciousness.

She allowed herself the luxury of closing her eyes, just for a few moments. When she opened them it was with a jolt that told her she'd nodded off.

Far too dangerous. She had to get out of the vehicle. She couldn't smell fuel but she wasn't taking chances. Suddenly Maggie realised in horror that she couldn't discern even the slightest movement from her baby.

Fear and guilt slashed at her. She should never have come alone. It didn't matter that she was a competent driver, well used to the roughest of roads. Fresh tears gathered, burning hot at the backs of her eyes, and she blinked them back. She had to move. Now.

Grasping the door handle up above her head, she tried to lever herself up.

Two things happened simultaneously. Pain shot through her left leg, strong enough to make her sway and the world recede for an instant. And she felt something else—a warm gush of liquid between her thighs.

Tentatively she reached down, dread icing her veins. But there was no mistaking it. Blood. Lots of it. She was bleeding and her baby was in danger.

Heedless of the pain that made her head reel, she reached out and hauled herself high enough to grasp the steering wheel. She jammed her fist down on the horn and kept it there.

CHAPTER FOURTEEN

HER impressions were jumbled. Above all there was pain and fear. Maggie heard voices, desperate, urgent voices, and felt hands, strong and sure on her body. There was a burst of sudden agony and nothing more.

Sounds roused her, the rapid thud, thud, thud almost deafening her. Was it her heartbeat pumping out the precious blood that her baby needed? Or was it a helicopter? Rescue? Maggie opened her mouth to ask, aware of a voice urgently calling her name, again and again. But no sound came and she slid back into the void of darkness.

It was pain that roused her once more. The pain of her fingers being squeezed so tight they would surely fuse together. Heat encompassed them, the living heat of a large, roughened hand. *Khalid*. He was there. He'd found her. Everything would be all right now.

Maggie struggled through the fog that trapped her, trying to reach him, give some response so he knew she was aware of him.

Voices reached her. Staccato orders from a voice she didn't recognise and, clashing across it, Khalid's hoarse, urgent tones. 'Do what you must. Anything you must, but save my wife. That's all that matters.'

For a brief moment longer Maggie fought to reach him, to connect with him, but the sounds of life slid away and she fell once more into the void.

When she finally came to, she felt…nothing. No hurt, no discomfort, nothing. She lay flat on her back. Her hand was warm where fingers held hers loosely.

Khalid. It was true, she thought muzzily. It hadn't been a dream. He'd been with her all this time.

Her limp body suffused with heat and something she was too weary to define. Relief? Love? Hope? She let the sensation wash through her, content that he was here.

Gradually her senses grew more alert as her body woke. Her eyelids flickered and her mouth twitched. She wanted to say his name, hear it powerful and real on her tongue.

Finally she found the energy, swallowing to moisten her dust-dry throat.

'Khalid,' she whispered. His name was like a talisman, the sound of it lending her strength to open her eyes.

'Maggie! Maggie, sweetheart, you're awake.' But it wasn't Khalid's velvet tones she heard. It was Zeinab.

Turning her head a fraction, she found her friend's face, watching her intently. The older woman seemed to have aged overnight and weariness lined her face.

'Everything's fine,' Zeinab assured her, though her eyes were shadowed and overbright. Maggie felt a thrill of instinctive fear claw at her. 'You're safe now.'

'The baby?' Her voice was a raw croak but Zeinab understood. She tipped her lips upwards in a taut smile.

'You have a little daughter, born by Caesarean section. She's in neonatal intensive care.'

Maggie's heart plummeted, a leaden weight as fear gripped her.

'How is she? *Really*?' Guilt racked her. It was her fault her baby had been born too early.

'She's small, so she needs extra attention. There were complications during the birth. But she's improving, growing stronger by the hour.'

Maggie stared into her friend's troubled eyes, trying to discern truth from optimistic assurance.

'Khalid has been with you all the time,' Zeinab said. 'He wouldn't leave your side. He's just gone to see the baby.'

But the platitudes didn't ring true. Tense as she was with fear for her daughter, her body exhausted, Maggie couldn't even summon the strength to be disappointed.

Khalid wasn't here and no amount of well-meaning assurances could hide that. Had Maggie really expected him to be at her side when she woke? She knew where his priorities lay, and that was with their child. It had always been the baby only that mattered to him.

Moisture gathered at the corners of her eyes and she turned her head towards the pillow, too weary to raise a hand and wipe it away as hurt filled her. Her heart squeezed, catching her breath against a pain that defied even the drugs filling her system.

She must have imagined the firm touch of his hand wrapping around hers. And his desperate voice imploring the medicos to save her.

Funny what the human brain could invent, wasn't it?

'Maggie.' Zeinab's voice was low and soothing. 'You and your little girl are safe in excellent hands here.' She paused as if searching for the right words. 'Khalid will be thrilled to see you conscious. He's been frantic about you both. But everything will be all right. You'll see.'

Maggie offered her friend a weak smile, but didn't say anything. What was there to say?

It was shatteringly clear that things would never be right, even if Zeinab was correct and her baby was safe. Oh, how she prayed Zeinab was right about that.

This marriage could never be fixed.

She closed her eyes and let herself slide back to that place where there was no pain and no disappointment, only the empty haven of darkness.

* * *

Khalid stood in the shadows of the dimly lit room and looked down into his wife's pale face.

The doctor's assurance that she'd already woken and was responding well didn't convince him. Fear gripped him in a vice. He wouldn't believe it till he saw for himself that she was recovering.

Only the exercise of supreme control held him still, knees locked, feet planted wide and hands clenched together behind his back.

He wanted to cradle her in his arms, kiss her back to consciousness, nuzzle the silken softness of her hair and whisper his regrets and his apologies. But he couldn't.

Guilt tore at him with razor-sharp talons, gnawed at his innards till only obstinate willpower kept him standing. *He'd* done this. Because of him Maggie had almost died, and their child with her.

He was to blame.

He'd thought he remembered the pain of loss but he hadn't been prepared for the ripping agony that had shredded him when he'd thought he was losing her. He should have been there to drive her, keep her safe.

More, he should never have agreed to a separation. He should have smashed through the barriers that divided them. Especially his own shameful denial of his feelings. He'd conditioned himself to believe he'd never again experience such emotions. He'd been a coward, afraid at the possibility of loving and losing again.

The rescue had been touch and go. It could easily have ended in disaster in that rugged terrain. The surgery had been a frantic attempt to save them both. Through it all Khalid had been useless, unable to do more than hold Maggie and cajole, plead, demand that she stay with him. The possibility that fate would steal her away had almost unmanned him. Even now fear trembled in his belly and hammered his pulse.

Her lashes moved, the shadows on her face shifting. Was she waking? He took a pace forward, then slammed to a halt as golden-green eyes fixed on him. The oxygen he'd inhaled disappeared and he grew dizzy with relief and remorse. She looked so fragile, so wan and helpless. He clasped his hands so hard they shook. But at least he was able to maintain a necessary distance. He had to respect her feelings, not bulldoze in and sweep her into his arms as he yearned to do.

'Khalid.' Her voice was bruised, a dry choking sob. He lunged forward and poured her water. She needed him. Any excuse to obliterate the distance between them.

'Here, *habibti*. Drink this.' He slid a hand behind her shoulders to lift her. She shuddered in his embrace and he hoped fervently it was from the physical effort. Not distaste.

Her lids lowered, her lashes concealing her expressive eyes as she then sank back. Reluctantly he eased her against the pillows and slid his hand away. His fingers flexed, warm with the feel of her delicate-boned body. He put the paper cup on the bedside table and forced himself to step away.

'How do you feel, Maggie?'

Her lips tilted up in a smile that wasn't a smile. 'Alive.'

'You had me worried.' The words burst from him. Worried...he'd been terrified!

Her eyes widened, rising to meet his. Then her gaze slid away. 'Yes, the baby. How is she?'

'Getting stronger all the time.' He'd been amazed at the tiny mite's resilience. It had given him strength when his own had begun to fail him. 'Beautiful like her mother.'

Again Maggie's eyes met his, just for an instant, and he read astonishment there.

'Really? She's safe?' she whispered.

Khalid nodded, seeing the echo of his own worry in her face. 'I promise. It hasn't been an easy start for her, but the signs are excellent and she's responding well. Here.' He allowed himself to step closer, fishing out his mobile phone. 'You'll want to see these.'

He flipped open the slimline phone and called up the photos he'd just taken. He handed it over, his momentary pleasure withering as he watched the way she studiously avoided touching him.

Ice clamped round his chest. He'd hurt her so badly, enough to make her run from him. He felt sick when he thought of her alone on the treacherous mountain road. Would she let him make reparation for his mistakes or was it too late?

No, he refused to countenance that possibility.

Her eyes fixed on the phone and her mouth opened on a sigh of astonished delight. Tenderness filled her eyes.

'She's gorgeous. And so tiny. Are you sure she'll be OK?'

He nodded. 'The doctors are very pleased with her progress.' No need to mention those first hours when the outlook had been grim indeed.

'I want to see her,' she whispered.

'You will. Soon.' He stood, frozen by the knowledge that he could have prevented this. If he hadn't let Maggie down, the pregnancy would have gone to term. She wouldn't have had to fight for her very life.

He hadn't been there. He hadn't earned her trust. He'd let their marriage disintegrate. No wonder she'd pushed him away. He'd taken her passion, her affection, even her innocence, and given nothing of substance in return. Nothing that truly mattered. No wonder she'd sought a chance to go out alone, escaping his company.

He was criminally culpable. Even if she could be persuaded to forgive him, he could never forgive himself.

Slowly he sank onto the seat by her bed. Was it imagination or did she lean away?

'Here. Thank you for showing me.'

She held out the phone and he shook his head. 'Keep it till you're able to see her.'

'Thank you.' Her voice was stilted as if she spoke to a stranger.

Khalid could bear it no longer.

'Maggie.' He reached for her hand, closing his fingers around it and holding firm though she tried to tug out of his grasp. His hold tightened reflexively. He never wanted to let her go.

Even now, here in the best hospital Shajehar boasted, he was terrified of losing her. He relived those moments when his world had tilted out of kilter and stopped. Maggie's scarf snapping from a rosebush like a banner in the breeze. The swelling roar of a vehicle engine as it departed the fortress. The metallic taste of terror burning his mouth as he realised Maggie was alone on the precarious mountain. The helplessness of waiting, praying for the chopper to arrive, knowing all he could do was hold her in his arms and not give up hope.

Echoes of the past had swamped him. He'd been terrified history was repeating itself.

'You're hurting me.'

Contrition filled him. Yet he couldn't release her. It was too much to ask.

'I'm sorry,' he murmured, lifting her hand and pressing tiny, fervent kisses to the back of it. She trembled in his hold.

'Please, Khalid.' She drew in a shaky breath so hard it rattled her chest. 'Please, don't.'

Her eyes were bright with tears and her mouth worked. Guilt scorched him. He didn't want to hurt her anymore.

'Don't cry, Maggie.' He turned over her hand and kissed her palm, inhaling her unique fragrance, recognisable despite the antiseptic hospital smells. He shut his eyes and breathed it in, then flicked out his tongue and tasted her. Reaction shuddered through him.

His woman. His. He would do anything for her but he wouldn't let her go. That was asking the impossible.

* * *

'I failed to protect you. Failed to protect my family.' Khalid's voice was tight, roughened as she'd never before heard it. His hand held hers in a steely grip and his face was grim.

His demeanour was starkly proprietorial. She sensed his control was skin-deep, a veneer of civilisation barely covering far more primitive instincts. Heat flared at that glimpse of untrammelled masculine possessiveness. But it wasn't for her. Would never be for her.

He'd feared for the baby. As she had. It was their one real emotional link: love of their child.

'It's all right, Khalid. It's over now. The baby is safe.' She didn't for an instant question the need to comfort him. She loved him, no matter that he didn't reciprocate her feelings.

'*You're* safe.' His voice was choked, thick with emotion and unfamiliar. 'I thought I'd lost you both.'

He raised his head and she was shocked by the raw emotion in his face. He looked ravaged by pain, the lines around his mouth scored deep; his eyes shimmered bright with anguish.

Her fingers curved around his, unhesitatingly offering comfort. She couldn't bear to see him in such agony.

'Seeing you there, unconscious.' He shook his head. 'It was like every nightmare of the past come to haunt me.'

The past? Of course, how could she have forgotten?

'Shahina,' she murmured dully. The accident must have sparked memories of his first wife's death.

He nodded, his mouth a line of twisted grief. 'How could I have let it happen? She died not ten kilometres from where you went off the road.'

Horror dried Maggie's mouth at the news. No wonder Khalid was distraught. What must he have gone through as he waited for help, wondering if the chopper would be on time?

'I should have known better than to take you into the mountains. Should have known it was too dangerous, especially for a pregnant woman. Too far from medical help.' He burrowed his fingers through his hair.

Maggie's distress and guilt seemed nothing to the agony she read in his eyes. Her heart twisted, wrung out by the emotion revealed there. Always Khalid had been controlled. Now she saw him stripped naked and grieving.

Instinctively Maggie lifted her hand to cup his jaw. Instantly he turned his face to nuzzle her palm, his long dark lashes sweeping down to hide his eyes. The rough texture of his chin grazed her and his moist hot breath hazed her sensitive skin.

'I don't deserve you, Maggie.'

Faced with his bone-deep pain, Maggie couldn't find it in her heart to be angry that he couldn't love her. Love wasn't a choice. It had come upon her out of the blue. She couldn't blame him for the fact that he'd given his heart years ago to another.

'I will never forgive myself. How can I expect you to forgive me?' His voice was a hollow groan. His lips moved against her skin as he anchored her cradling palm against his face with his hand.

'Khalid—'

'But I have to ask. I *must*.'

'Khalid, there's nothing to forgive.'

'Isn't there?' His eyes snapped open to ensnare hers. 'What about our marriage?'

'Please, don't,' she begged, trying to keep her voice steady. She didn't have the stamina to hear him put it into words. That their marriage was a mistake. That his heart belonged to his first wife.

Had he changed his mind about divorce? Legally she'd be free then. But Maggie knew in her aching soul that she'd never be whole again.

His eyes didn't leave hers. 'I must speak, Maggie. I have been remiss. Worse than that. I made you miserable.' He gathered in an enormous breath that hefted his shoulders and chest high.

'I've been content for too long to enjoy the benefits of marriage, the benefits of you—' his eyes narrowed '—without giving all of myself in return. I've been utterly selfish. I kept my emotional distance because I didn't believe I could love again. You deserve more than that.'

He was about to give her the freedom she needed. So why did she feel like a doomed prisoner, awaiting a death sentence?

Hot tears glazed the backs of her eyes and she tried to tug her hand free of his grip. She needed space. She needed to be alone.

But he wouldn't relinquish his hold.

'It wasn't till you stood up to me, till you denied me your body, *more*, your affection, that I realised what I'd done. That's when I understood what I felt for you.'

Maggie's breath came in short, sharp pants as her chest constricted. Yet she was powerless to turn away from his dark-as-night eyes, so brilliant and intent.

'I'm ashamed, Maggie. Truly ashamed, that I didn't understand before.' He shook his head. 'I hid from the truth, too cowardly to see beyond the narrow limits I'd set. I should have realised how badly I treated you.' His hand tightened on hers as his voice cracked.

'Khalid. No more. Please. I know how you feel; you don't need to say any more.' Already her heart was splintering as pain lanced her.

'Then you are far more insightful than I am, *habibti*. It took me too long to understand what you meant to me. How I'd grown to love you for your strength and beauty, your charm and tenderness, your warmth, your determination, all the things that make you the special woman you are.'

Maggie could only stare, meeting Khalid's eyes and seeing the honesty etched there.

'I thought it was convenience, liking, respect, even cataclysmic sexual need, that kept me wanting to be with you,' he continued. 'Anything except love.'

Love?

Maggie gaped, bereft of words.

'It was easier to tell myself I desired you because you were so sexy, any man's fantasy,' he murmured between fervent kisses to her palm. 'Or that you were good company, able to listen and give another perspective on problems. Or that I respected the way you adapted to the demands of life in a new country.'

'Or that I carried your baby?' She couldn't accept his wonderful words, despite the hope burgeoning inside her.

He nodded. 'That was another logical reason, that you were pregnant with our child. After all, it was the excuse I used to force you into marriage.'

'Excuse?' She frowned.

'I'd already decided I wanted you in my life. Your pregnancy forced my hand, but I didn't regret it.' He smiled, a flash of sheer exuberant masculine pleasure that rocked all her senses. 'I knew after one night I wanted much more from you. I had no intention of being denied. That's why you were brought to Shajehar. I had every intention of seducing you into my bed again and again.'

Heat flared in his lustrous eyes and Maggie felt an answering spark deep inside. But it was too much to take in. Too much to believe. She turned her face away.

'No, Khalid. There's no need to lie, to hide the truth.' He was trying to build something between them that just wasn't there. Presumably for their baby's sake.

'The truth? The truth is that I adore you, *habibti*. I have done for months, but I was too blind and obstinate to see. Hussein knew. And Zeinab. But they kept their counsel until Hussein confronted me at the fortress.'

'Hussein said he'd seen you and Shahina together and that I deserved to know the truth.' There. She'd said it, brought the spectre of his one true love into the open. She stared at her free hand, pleating the edge of the sheet.

'Ah, so you heard that?'

Miserably she nodded. 'You said I was different to Shahina. That you felt the difference every time you saw me.'

She sank her teeth into her cheek to prevent her jaw from wobbling. She would *not* break down.

'Exactly so, my sweet.' His hand was a hot caress tilting her chin up. Through the haze of her pain Maggie registered the tremor in his fingers.

'Shahina was my first love. We'd known each other all our lives and fell into romance almost as part of growing up. What we had was special and I never thought to experience love for another woman again.'

She could barely breathe when he looked at her like that.

'I never expected to be swept away by a love so powerful it played havoc with my common sense, as well as my libido. To find a woman who means more to me than life itself.' His fingers stroked, feather-light, across her lips. 'Yes, I loved Shahina, but you made me realise that I had to move on from the past. I love you, Maggie, with all my being. This is like a lightning bolt that has pierced my heart. I'm no callow youth and I know what I want in my life.' He drew in a shuddering breath.

'I want you. Always. For ever. Is it possible you feel something, *anything*, for me? Enough to accept my apology and stay?'

Her eyes glazed with tears. She so wanted it to be true. 'That's shock talking. The accident reminded you of Shahina.'

The horror on his face stilled her breathing. 'No, my love. Never say that! Despite the memories, my fear was all for you. And our child. What I feel for you is real and true.' He swallowed convulsively. 'Without you, I am nothing. I am the dust beneath your feet.'

He leaned in and pressed his lips to hers, in a tender kiss that made her heart flip over. 'But I heard—'

'You heard my uncle berating me for letting our marriage continue in stalemate. I'd only just realised my feelings for you. And understood how little I'd given you in return for your faith and loyalty and passion. I was racked by guilt.' His gaze held her spellbound for so long she was sure he could read her emotions clear in her eyes.

'I knew I was in love, that you were the most precious thing in my world. That I could never bear to lose you. The knowledge scared me witless. You'd withdrawn from me, with good reason. I had no idea how to persuade you to trust me, to give me another chance.'

He cupped her face with both hands. 'I wish I'd done it differently. I would have courted you properly, told you I loved you. Instead I was paralysed, fearing I'd pushed you too far. That I didn't have a hope of winning you.' He shuddered and closed his eyes.

'Khalid.' His name had never tasted so perfect on her lips. She stared, wondering, at the man who for the first time revealed his innermost fears and hopes in his unguarded eyes.

'Can you forgive me, Maggie? For not deserving you? For not offering you my love earlier? I hurt you so badly.' Desperation coloured his voice. A stark fear that matched the blaze of emotion in his eyes.

'Hush.' Her fingers were unsteady as she pressed them to his lips. Inside she felt a warmth unfurl and spread through her whole being. The warmth of love such as she'd never known in all her days.

'There's nothing to forgive, Khalid.'

His gaze trapped her, so intense it branded her.

'Maggie. You can't mean that.'

Tentatively she smiled, blinking back tears as she met his hopeful, longing look.

'I do.' It was all she could manage as her throat closed.

'Then tell me. Tell me what I need to hear.' There was a hint of his old autocratic tone in his velvet-deep voice as he stared down at her. A hint of imperiousness in the tilt of his head. But the uncertainty she read in his eyes belied his show of arrogance. It convinced her as no words could have done.

'I love you, Khalid,' she said for the first time, hearing the joy and wonder of it in her voice, seeing it reflected in his loving expression.

Then he pulled her close and there were no more words for a very long time.

CHAPTER FIFTEEN

MAGGIE bade farewell to the last of the tribal women at the door of the walled garden. The meeting had gone well and they'd been enthusiastic about the new school in the valley. One of them had even broached the possibility of a literacy programme for adults. Maggie smiled as she turned and made her way back through the scented garden.

Khalid had already battled hard to ensure that the more traditional local elders hadn't vetoed the idea of girls attending the school. He would have to be his most persuasive to convince them that their wives should also learn. But Maggie had no doubts her husband would prevail. He could be so persuasive when he wished. Or downright autocratic if the occasion demanded.

A frisson of delicious heat spiralled through her and she paused, sidetracked by the idea of him being persuasive.

'What are you smiling about, *habibti*?'

She turned to find him emerging from the shadows. The sun glinted off his hair with the blue-black sheen of a raven's wing. It gilded his compellingly handsome features and highlighted the tiny laughter lines around his mouth and eyes. She loved his laugh, rich and so mellow it always seemed to rumble right through her.

Her gaze traced his lean, sculpted features, his powerful

shoulders and dropped to the burden he cradled so easily yet so protectively in his arms.

Jasmine was six months old, round-cheeked and button-nosed. She had dark hair like her father and a rich little chuckle that suited her sunny temperament. Right now she had the fidgety look of a hungry baby.

As ever, the sight of them together, the two people in the world who meant everything to her, made her heart turn over in her chest.

She watched Khalid tuck their daughter further into the curve of his arm and knew how lucky she was. He was everything she wanted in a man, a husband, a lover, a father for her child.

'I was just thinking of how good you are at getting your own way when you want something, Your Majesty.' She lowered her eyes in a deliberately flirtatious move.

'That's it. Pander to my fantasy that I'm in total control of my own household.' She heard the amusement in his voice. 'But it seems to me that you're the persuasive one. Who was it that decided we should spend a few months each year here in the mountains?'

She looked up. The warmth of his gaze squeezed her insides as it always did when he looked at her with love in his eyes.

'Do you regret it?'

He shook his head. 'No. You were right. I can't keep you and Jasmine coddled in cotton wool, much as I'd like to.' He drew Maggie close with his free arm, his lips a temptation to surrender as he nibbled at her neck.

'Khalid!'

'Hmm?'

Maggie tried in vain to ignore the glorious sensations his caress engendered. She reached for Jasmine, who gurgled her approval. The warm baby scent filled her nostrils as Maggie cradled her.

'This isn't the time or the place,' she said, trying to sound sensible.

'Perhaps you're right.' He glanced down as Jasmine plucked hungrily at the silk of Maggie's bodice. 'This isn't the time. But after you've fed Jasmine, perhaps you'll let me practise those skills of persuasion on you.' His sleek brows tilted up in a lascivious waggle that did nothing to detract from his sheer physical magnetism.

He curved his arms lightly around her and Jasmine, holding them in his strong, protective embrace.

Maggie sighed with pure delight. She'd found the love she'd never thought would be hers. She had everything her heart desired.

Dreams really did come true.

AUGUST 2008 HARDBACK TITLES

ROMANCE

Virgin for the Billionaire's Taking   978 0 263 20334 9
Penny Jordan
Purchased: His Perfect Wife *Helen Bianchin*   978 0 263 20335 6
The Vasquez Mistress *Sarah Morgan*   978 0 263 20336 3
At the Sheikh's Bidding *Chantelle Shaw*   978 0 263 20337 0
The Spaniard's Marriage Bargain *Abby Green*   978 0 263 20338 7
Sicilian Millionaire, Bought Bride   978 0 263 20339 4
Catherine Spencer
Italian Prince, Wedlocked Wife *Jennie Lucas*   978 0 263 20340 0
The Desert King's Pregnant Bride *Annie West* 978 0 263 20341 7
Bride at Briar's Ridge *Margaret Way*   978 0 263 20342 4
Last-Minute Proposal *Jessica Hart*   978 0 263 20343 1
The Single Mum and the Tycoon   978 0 263 20344 8
Caroline Anderson
Found: His Royal Baby *Raye Morgan*   978 0 263 20345 5
The Millionaire's Nanny Arrangement   978 0 263 20346 2
Linda Goodnight
Hired: The Boss's Bride *Ally Blake*   978 0 263 20347 9
A Boss Beyond Compare *Dianne Drake*   978 0 263 20348 6
The Emergency Doctor's Chosen Wife   978 0 263 20349 3
Molly Evans

HISTORICAL

Scandalising the Ton *Diane Gaston*   978 0 263 20207 6
Her Cinderella Season *Deb Marlowe*   978 0 263 20208 3
The Warrior's Princess Bride *Meriel Fuller*   978 0 263 20209 0

MEDICAL™

A Baby for Eve *Maggie Kingsley*   978 0 263 19906 2
Marrying the Millionaire Doctor *Alison Roberts* 978 0 263 19907 9
His Very Special Bride *Joanna Neil*   978 0 263 19908 6
City Surgeon, Outback Bride *Lucy Clark*   978 0 263 19909 3

MILLS & BOON®
Pure reading pleasure™

AUGUST 2008 LARGE PRINT TITLES

ROMANCE

The Italian Billionaire's Pregnant Bride *Lynne Graham*	978 0 263 20066 9
The Guardian's Forbidden Mistress *Miranda Lee*	978 0 263 20067 6
Secret Baby, Convenient Wife *Kim Lawrence*	978 0 263 20068 3
Caretti's Forced Bride *Jennie Lucas*	978 0 263 20069 0
The Bride's Baby *Liz Fielding*	978 0 263 20070 6
Expecting a Miracle *Jackie Braun*	978 0 263 20071 3
Wedding Bells at Wandering Creek *Patricia Thayer*	978 0 263 20072 0
The Loner's Guarded Heart *Michelle Douglas*	978 0 263 20073 7

HISTORICAL

Lady Gwendolen Investigates *Anne Ashley*	978 0 263 20163 5
The Unknown Heir *Anne Herries*	978 0 263 20164 2
Forbidden Lord *Helen Dickson*	978 0 263 20165 9

MEDICAL™

The Doctor's Bride By Sunrise *Josie Metcalfe*	978 0 263 19968 0
Found: A Father For Her Child *Amy Andrews*	978 0 263 19969 7
A Single Dad at Heathermere *Abigail Gordon*	978 0 263 19970 3
Her Very Special Baby *Lucy Clark*	978 0 263 19971 0
The Heart Surgeon's Secret Son *Janice Lynn*	978 0 263 19972 7
The Sheikh Surgeon's Proposal *Olivia Gates*	978 0 263 19973 4

MILLS & BOON®
Pure reading pleasure™

SEPTEMBER 2008 HARDBACK TITLES

ROMANCE

Ruthlessly Bedded by the Italian Billionaire *Emma Darcy*	978 0 263 20350 9
Mendez's Mistress *Anne Mather*	978 0 263 20351 6
Rafael's Suitable Bride *Cathy Williams*	978 0 263 20352 3
Desert Prince, Defiant Virgin *Kim Lawrence*	978 0 263 20353 0
Sicilian Husband, Unexpected Baby *Sharon Kendrick*	978 0 263 20354 7
Hired: The Italian's Convenient Mistress *Carol Marinelli*	978 0 263 20355 4
Antonides' Forbidden Wife *Anne McAllister*	978 0 263 20356 1
The Millionaire's Chosen Bride *Susanne James*	978 0 263 20357 8
Wedded in a Whirlwind *Liz Fielding*	978 0 263 20358 5
Blind Date with the Boss *Barbara Hannay*	978 0 263 20359 2
The Tycoon's Christmas Proposal *Jackie Braun*	978 0 263 20360 8
Christmas Wishes, Mistletoe Kisses *Fiona Harper*	978 0 263 20361 5
Rescued by the Magic of Christmas *Melissa McClone*	978 0 263 20362 2
Her Millionaire, His Miracle *Myrna Mackenzie*	978 0 263 20363 9
Italian Doctor, Sleigh-Bell Bride *Sarah Morgan*	978 0 263 20364 6
The Desert Surgeon's Secret Son *Olivia Gates*	978 0 263 20365 3

HISTORICAL

Scandalous Secret, Defiant Bride *Helen Dickson*	978 0 263 20210 6
A Question of Impropriety *Michelle Styles*	978 0 263 20211 3
Conquering Knight, Captive Lady *Anne O'Brien*	978 0 263 20212 0

MEDICAL™

Dr Devereux's Proposal *Margaret McDonagh*	978 0 263 19910 9
Children's Doctor, Meant-to-be Wife *Meredith Webber*	978 0 263 19911 6
Christmas at Willowmere *Abigail Gordon*	978 0 263 19912 3
Dr Romano's Christmas Baby *Amy Andrews*	978 0 263 19913 0

MILLS & BOON™®

Pure reading pleasure™

SEPTEMBER 2008 LARGE PRINT TITLES

ROMANCE

The Markonos Bride *Michelle Reid*	978 0 263 20074 4
The Italian's Passionate Revenge *Lucy Gordon*	978 0 263 20075 1
The Greek Tycoon's Baby Bargain *Sharon Kendrick*	978 0 263 20076 8
Di Cesare's Pregnant Mistress *Chantelle Shaw*	978 0 263 20077 5
His Pregnant Housekeeper *Caroline Anderson*	978 0 263 20078 2
The Italian Playboy's Secret Son *Rebecca Winters*	978 0 263 20079 9
Her Sheikh Boss *Carol Grace*	978 0 263 20080 5
Wanted: White Wedding *Natasha Oakley*	978 0 263 20081 2

HISTORICAL

The Last Rake In London *Nicola Cornick*	978 0 263 20166 6
The Outrageous Lady Felsham *Louise Allen*	978 0 263 20167 3
An Unconventional Miss *Dorothy Elbury*	978 0 263 20168 0

MEDICAL™

The Surgeon's Fatherhood Surprise *Jennifer Taylor*	978 0 263 19974 1
The Italian Surgeon Claims His Bride *Alison Roberts*	978 0 263 19975 8
Desert Doctor, Secret Sheikh *Meredith Webber*	978 0 263 19976 5
A Wedding in Warragurra *Fiona Lowe*	978 0 263 19977 2
The Firefighter and the Single Mum *Laura Iding*	978 0 263 19978 9
The Nurse's Little Miracle *Molly Evans*	978 0 263 19979 6